Fifteen Modern Tales of Attraction

By the same author

The Changeling
The Wave Theory of Angels

Fifteen Modern Tales
of Attraction

ALISON MACLEOD

HAMISH HAMILTON
an imprint of
PENGUIN BOOKS

HAMISH HAMILTON

Published by the Penguin Group
Penguin Books Ltd, 80 Strand, London WC2R ORL, England
Penguin Group (USA) Inc., 375 Hudson Street, New York, New York 10014, USA
Penguin Group (Canada), 90 Eglinton Avenue East, Suite 700, Toronto, Ontario, Canada M4P 2Y3
(a division of Pearson Penguin Canada Inc.)
Penguin Ireland, 25 St Stephen's Green, Dublin 2, Ireland
(a division of Penguin Books Ltd)
Penguin Group (Australia), 250 Camberwell Road, Camberwell, Victoria 3124, Australia
(a division of Pearson Australia Group Pty Ltd)
Penguin Books India Pvt Ltd, 11 Community Centre, Panchsheel Park, New Delhi – 110 017, India
Penguin Group (NZ), 67 Apollo Drive, Rosedale, North Shore 0632, New Zealand
(a division of Pearson New Zealand Ltd)
Penguin Books (South Africa) (Pty) Ltd, 24 Sturdee Avenue,
Rosebank, Johannesburg 2196, South Africa

Penguin Books Ltd, Registered Offices: 80 Strand, London WC2R ORL, England

www.penguin.com

First published 2007

1

Set in 11/13 pt Monotype Dante
Typeset by Rowland Phototypesetting Ltd, Bury St Edmunds, Suffolk
Printed in Great Britain by Clays Ltd, St Ives plc

A CIP catalogue record for this book is available from the British Library

ISBN: 978-0-241-14262-2

For Hugh Dunkerley and Hugo Donnelly

Acknowledgements

I would like to thank my talented editors at Hamish Hamilton, Juliette Mitchell, Simon Prosser and Francesca Main, who, year on year, bring exciting new literature into the world against the odds. I am grateful, too, to my agent, David Godwin, for his high energy and know-how. I'd also like to thank my reader-friends Hugh Dunkerley, Karen Stevens and Jane Rusbridge.

Grateful acknowledgement is made to the following for permission to include previously published stories: *Prospect* for 'Sacred Heart' and 'Radiant Heat' (in which the character of Kurt Zucker is very loosely based on the quantum physicist Klaus Kinder-Geiger, who was killed in the Swissair crash that took place just beyond Halifax, Nova Scotia, in 1998; Zucker's personal life, however, is entirely fictional); Pulp.Net for 'Life and Soul' and 'Discharge'; *London Magazine* for 'Live Wire'; Virago for 'Rosie's Tongue', from their collection *Short Circuits*; and Littlewood Press for 'Where there is milk, where there is honey', originally entitled 'Simon S-S-Says', from their collection *Northern Stories*; also to Picador Books for allowing me to use Kathleen Jamie's poem, 'The Creel', and to General Motors for my use of some of their advertising detail in 'The Will Writer'.

Contents

so that the land was darkened

1. August 1999

'Race me,' you said that day at the bottom of Bow Hill.

We collapsed on the grassy height, our chests heaving, while, over the Atlantic, the shadow of the moon sped towards us at 1,500 miles per hour. Like all the others that day, we'd climbed through the yew wood to the top of the hill, and then higher still, to the top of one of the ancient barrows, where we'd staked our claim, spreading a blanket and cracking open bottles of cool spring water. In the ground beneath us, the Bronze Age dead slept on. Poor buggers, I thought. Poor buggers – what they wouldn't give.

I walked to the edge of the barrow. Far below, wheat fields stretched away in tawny flanks of stubble, while, in the distance, the coastal plain of West Sussex shimmered, illusory in the light of mid-August.

'Nathan!' you called. 'Almost time.'

I lowered the binoculars, returned to our patch, and looped my yellow eclipse-glasses over my ears.

'*Sex-y*,' you pronounced.

'I rather thought that might be the case,' I replied, my eyebrow cocked. Then I pushed you on to the mildewed blanket and kissed you, our noses and glasses bumping. Even as we kissed, they were ringing temple bells in India and beating steel plates with sticks. They were going cold at the sight of black chicks hatched that morning. They were ushering children and pregnant women indoors. Within the hour, they'd be washing down their walls, cleaning them of the breath of darkness.

You and I, we hardly saw it coming.

I

'Quick!' you cried, peering out from under me. 'We're missing it.' High above Bow Hill, the sky had dimmed and the moon had started to eat the sun. We sat up and turned our faces skywards. The scattered schoolchildren started to clap – too early in their eagerness.

'Over here,' called their teacher, and he gathered them all just behind us. around a simple pinhole projector. Soon they were sitting quietly, mesmerized by the progress of the shadow they'd trapped in the cardboard box.

'Better, sir,' piped up one, 'than watching the old cricket my sister has at home in a jam jar.'

It could have been me fifteen years before. 'Swot,' I mumbled – under my breath, I could have sworn.

'Plonker,' came the swot's reply.

'Geek,' I insisted, not taking my eyes off the sun.

'Alpha geek,' he countered, hardly turning.

'Nerd,' I whispered hotly.

'Nutter,' he retorted coolly.

'Propellerhead,' I tried.

'Four eyes,' he fired.

I pushed my flimsy glasses up the bridge of my nose. What could I do but concede the point?

You tapped the victor's scrawny back. He turned, uncertain. Smiling, you passed him a melting HobNob from the stash in your rucksack. And it was obvious – from the way his fingers hovered in mid-air, from the sudden glassy look in his beady eyes, from the bubble of saliva on his lower lip – that he'd fallen helplessly in love with you.

I knew the feeling. Hadn't I tripped up the steps of the British Museum the first time I saw you?

You were sitting on the fourth step from the top, your skirt spread wide, your legs bare and your head thrown back to the sun, like an acolyte on a fag break outside the temple. It was

June 21st. The first day of summer. In less than two months, we'd be together on top of Bow Hill.

I steadied myself, walked up the remaining steps, and hovered painfully at the museum's main doors. I looked at my watch. Six minutes late for work already. Any longer would require fast talking – never my forte.

Yet I drew breath and walked back down. 'Hello,' I said. A clear opening line. A perfectly adequate opening line.

You turned slowly towards me, your eyes squinting against the midday light – blue eyes, lit from behind in that strange Celtic way – and my heart wrecked as I heard myself. 'I want you to know that I haven't been watching you, which isn't to say I don't regret the lack of opportunity, though I'm not a perve – you have my word on that – and, it's true, you could be awful and I could be badly mistaken, but I think the opposite might be the case, which is to say, I think you're probably lovely – I mean I can *see* you're lovely, no probably about it – which is, in any case, why I'm standing here embarrassing myself when really I should be back at work by now, blowing the dust off some clay beaker – I work here' – I waved a hand at the main doors – 'but I find myself standing – no, loitering – beside you with something tantamount to verbal constipation, trying to ask you if you would agree to have coffee with me while also hoping you're not about to call Security, and that, if nothing else, you have at least, please God, a working knowledge of English.'

Eyes the colour of lapis lazuli.

'I'd need a lot more than a working knowledge,' you said, and you looked away again. American. Or Canadian. A tourist. A short-term visitor. Gone in two weeks. Or two days. I could hardly bear it.

'Yes,' I stammered. 'Of course. Absolutely. And apologies. I *am* a prat, though I have it on reliable authority that, when all's said and done, I really am quite okay.'

'Really quite okay,' you repeated, inscrutable.

'Yes.' Oh God. 'Really.'

You shielded your eyes with your hand. 'So is it coffee in clay beakers then?'

Was that a yes? 'Um, no. But I know a place that does a good line in polystyrene.'

You weren't sure.

Keep talking, I told myself. 'Cups which, no doubt, will be part of the archaeological horde the next millennials are doomed to unearth.'

You looked up. 'They don't biodegrade?'

'Not in a time known to man.'

'Oh . . .'

I was losing you. 'Then again, there's a tearoom not far from here. Sweaty scones, grumpy service, good bone china.'

You smiled at the step below you. You didn't make sense. You were North American but you were noticeably shy. There was a travel journal – pages of tight, cramped writing – flapping in the breeze beside you, yet you idled on the steps of the BM as if you'd never been anywhere else; as if you'd just walked free of some classical frieze. You were long-limbed – statuesque rather than slender – and your feet (bare, sandal-free), I suddenly noticed, were surprisingly large. Incongruously large. In fact, I'd never seen such big feet on a woman. Lord. How odd. But didn't Botticelli's Venus also have unusually sturdy feet?

You must have noticed me noticing because, suddenly, you pulled them protectively close. Yet, the truth was, I wanted nothing more than to cup the travelling sole of one of those feet in my hand.

The urge made me reckless. 'Meet me at the Elgin Marbles at five.'

You drilled the step with your big toe. 'Five it is,' you said at last.

'I'm Nathan,' I said.

You nodded to the main doors. 'You're late.'

At the top of Bow Hill, perched high on our burial mound, I hauled you between my legs and gathered you to my chest. The light turned briefly golden, the honeyed light of a late-summer's afternoon. You leaned your head in the cradle of my neck, and we watched the vast V-shaped shadow of the moon cross the fields below. It was a panorama I had known as long as I could remember. 'My family had a summer cottage not far from here,' I said. 'Mouldering, year in, year out.'

You crunched on an apple. 'Your family or the cottage?'

'Both, as it happens.'

You turned round, your eyes bright, searching.

I shrugged. 'I used to escape to up here.'

Below us, on the hill's plateau, a special-needs carer was running after her charge – a laughing girl with a collapsed face, a jutting nose and a crone's chin. Or was she a laughing crone with the slim build and friskiness of a girl? As I watched she metamorphosed back and forth, back and forth, like a Victorian reversible illustration. The wind came up. The sky deepened to purple. I rubbed the goose-pimples on your bare arms. Overhead, swallows darted and dived in the mistaken twilight, raking the air for insects that weren't there.

My mouth was next to your ear. 'Will we do this again in eighty-two years?'

'See you here,' you whispered back.

Far beneath us, the tribal chieftains were dreaming of Bronze Age bling: copper daggers, votive shields, capes of gold. Behind us, a few of the schoolchildren giggled with sudden nerves. You squeezed my knee. I kissed your neck. The rare wew-wew-wew chur-chur of a nightingale rippled on the air. Then, high above us, someone blew out the candle of the day.

11. August 2003

Toronto brought out the worst in me.

It was hot. Thirty-two degrees. I wanted only the deep, wood-wormy gloom of a pub somewhere on the Downs.

It didn't help that every Canadian man was three times broader than I was. Or that their teeth were disconcertingly white. Or that in every bar, every café, they stared openly at you, smiling, as if to say, '*You*? With *him*?' And contrary to what I'd been guaranteed by many a London friend, everyone didn't love my accent. Moreover, in exile from WC1, I could suddenly hear why. I sounded stiff. Lofty. I sounded like I was up to something.

'I'm just making a suggestion, Nathan. It's three-thirty and we haven't been anywhere yet. *Why* don't you want to go to the CN Tower? The views up there are really something.'

'Vertigo,' I said. I looked about in my desultory way. 'Why is there no litter in Toronto?'

'Because there isn't.'

'It's almost eerie.'

'You're almost eerie. What about Casa Loma? The gardens . . . ?'

'Crowds.'

'A boat tour of the islands?'

'Seasickness.'

You toed the sewer grate with your tremendous foot. Next to you, suddenly, I felt small and mean, and meaner still as you smiled and slapped your thigh in that Doris Day way of yours. 'Out with it,' you said. 'What do you want to do?'

'Honestly?'

'Honestly.'

'You won't mind?' The devil on my shoulder was taking hold.

'I won't mind.'

My finger stabbed the map. 'I rather fancy the Shoe Museum.'

You blinked. 'The Shoe Museum?'

'Yup. That's the ticket.'

Because shoes made you self-conscious.

I picked up the sheet of trivia on our way in. 'What was the most ever paid for a pair of used shoes?'

'Don't know.'

'Eight pairs of ruby slippers were made for Judy Garland for *The Wizard of Oz*. The last pair were auctioned for $665,000.'

'Who would have guessed?'

'"One small step for man, one giant leap for mankind."'

'Neil Armstrong.'

'Of course it's Neil Armstrong. Nineteen sixty-nine. Everyone knows that. But where are his boots from that very first moonwalk?'

'Here at the Shoe Museum!'

'Wrong. They were jettisoned from Apollo before returning to earth in case of contamination.'

'Oh.'

'Approximately what percentage of all the bones in the human body are found in the foot?'

'Nathan, can we *look* at something now?'

'One quarter – or, a little more in your case.'

You looked up, your eyes narrowing.

We stared at ancient funerary sandals. We pondered a range of silk 'pedestal' shoes. You liked the nineteenth-century Peruvian woman's silver stirrups. You tried to imagine me in the Argentinian rawhide gaucho boots. We both fell quiet before a pair of beaded shoes from Persia, dating from 1830. Inside, on the insole, a blessing had been inscribed for the wearer. 'In the name of Allah, the all merciful, the all compassionate. May all your needs be near. May your love of this little life carry you far.'

'Every shoe should say that,' you said quietly.

7

'Every shoe should,' I agreed.

We arrived at the exhibition of shoes for bound feet. Shoes, some no longer than three inches, seemed as if they'd been made for a toddler's foot. Yet they were exquisite: silk-covered, finely embroidered, fantastical in shape. Green for celebration. 'Red, apparently, for the bedroom.'

You looked up. 'They're awful . . . They shouldn't be –'

I read aloud from my fact sheet: ' "The practice of foot-binding originated in the eleventh century with the Chinese upper classes. It is estimated that, by the end of the nineteenth century, some 100 million women had had their feet broken and bound, often by their own mothers so they might attract a good class of suitor. Moreover, it was generally believed that the binding of the foot produced a tighter genital region." ' I looked at you over the sheet and choked back a witticism. ' "The four little toes were bent under the foot and bound, leaving the big toe pointing forward. Toes and heel were forced together. Toenails sometimes grew into the soles of the feet. The arch would grow so high, the toes often broke as a result. The process could take up to three years and began when girls were as young as two." ' I drew breath and looked up again. 'Gosh. Your mum would have had her work cut out –'

My smile died. Your eyes were glacial.

Then gone.

The lights were out. All of them. The overhead lighting. The display case lighting. The exit signs.

'Laura?' I called into the low-ceilinged dark. I edged my way along the wall and around a corner. 'Laura!'

An attendant appeared with a torch. 'Sir, I'm afraid I'll have to ask you to exit the building now. We're experiencing a power failure.'

'I gathered.' Was he fifteen or did he only look fifteen?

'So I'll have to ask you to leave the building for your own safety.'

'And you'll have my full cooperation just as soon as I locate my girlfriend.'

He shone his torch around the room. 'She's not here.'

'Hence my difficulty in finding her.'

'If she's anywhere, she'll be outside by now.'

'What do you mean, "if" she's anywhere?' I couldn't stop myself. 'Do you think I'm referring to my *imaginary* girlfriend?'

His boyish lips twitched. I folded my arms and held my ground. Or did, rather, until it struck him: one doesn't have to negotiate with screwballs. 'If you'll just follow me, sir,' he said. Then he too was gone, the light of his torch bobbing at speed into the distance.

I caught sight of you just before you turned from Bloor on to Spadina. 'Laura!' I called. 'Wait!'

You didn't.

It was two blocks before I caught you up. 'I'm sorry,' I wheezed. 'I'm really sorry.'

'Bully for you.' You wouldn't slow down. Your cheeks were blotchy with anger and heat.

'Didn't I tell you? The day we met?'

'Didn't you tell me what?'

'I'm a prat. I could have sworn I told you.'

You turned to me, briefly. Your eyes were filling.

'Laura, I'm sorry. I really am.'

'What's *wrong* with you today?'

'Nothing's wrong with me. I'm just . . . hot. That's all.'

You were outwalking me again.

Say it. Just say it, nimrod. 'I'm jealous!' I called.

A bloke walking past laughed into his takeaway coffee.

You stopped and wiped your nose with your wrist. 'Jealous? What do you mean, "jealous"?'

'What people usually mean, I guess.'

'Are you crazy?'

'Possibly.'

'Jealous of who, for Pete's sake?'

I shrugged. 'Of you.'

'Of *me*? Of me *how*?'

I smiled feebly at the pavement. 'You're too lovely.'

You rolled your eyes.

'You're too well adjusted.' I could hear myself, jingling all the loose change in my pockets. 'You're too *kind*.'

You rubbed the sweat from your forehead.

'And when you finally realize how lovely you actually are – which I don't let you know about often enough for fear you will – you'll leave me. You'll come back here, to this pure and litterless land, and I'll never see you again.'

You sighed and looked at the pavement. 'Prat.'

'You'll find I do answer to it.'

You walked tentatively towards me. 'The power's out.'

'So I'm told.'

Your hand found mine. 'I mean everywhere.'

And for the first time, I looked around. The traffic lights were out. There was a tailback of cars stretching back to Bloor and beyond. In the distance, there was a stranded streetcar. Horns were honking. A few brave Torontonians were venturing on to the street to direct traffic.

I started walking. 'Come on. I know a much nicer place than the Shoe Museum.'

'Nathan, you know the airport.'

'May all your needs be near . . .'

You smiled reluctantly. 'May your love of this little life carry you far.'

Bloor and Spadina. By the Jewish Community Centre. I'd remembered rightly. Greg's Ice Cream.

Nor were my calculations in vain. The freezer was out of action. The air conditioning was down. A queue was already forming at the door. Between the power outage and the heat, they couldn't give the stuff away fast enough.

'Organic,' said the lad behind the counter. His silver scoop was a blur of action. 'No preservatives. No fixing agents. In an hour, maybe less, we'll be at frigging sea in here.'

Madagascar Vanilla. Extreme Chocolate. Peachy Keen. Coffee Toffee. Crème Caramel. Irish Cream. Champagne. You ordered two scoops of Roasted Marshmallow. I fancied the Figs and Port. 'Straight up,' I said.

'Huh?' said the lad.

'He'd like it in a dish. Two scoops. No cone.'

'No *cone*?' Again that look: you're *with* this guy? But you reached for my arm, pulling it across your back and around your waist, in spite of the heat.

Every cellphone network was jammed. The queue at the phone box outside was ten-people deep. There wasn't a bank machine in the city that was working. News blew in like tumbleweed off the street. The power failure was bigger than Toronto, someone said. Bigger than Ontario. At eleven past four that afternoon, twenty-one power plants had gone down, as far south as New Jersey and as far west as Ohio.

A fire at a nuclear power station in Pennsylvania was to blame. No, it was a lightning strike at a generating station in Niagara Falls, someone said. 'Could even be a goddamned squirrel that found its way on to the grid,' said one of Greg's customers from behind the *Star*. Whatever the cause, the whole of the Eastern Grid had toppled. Fifty million people in Canada and the US were without power. It was the biggest blackout in the history of the continent.

At a table across from ours, a middle-aged couple turned up the volume on a wind-up radio. An energy consultant was speaking on CBC. 'Minutes before it collapsed,' he said, 'the grid experienced a dramatic loss of voltage. That triggered automatic switches that shut down all the major power plants within just nine seconds. Like it or not, we're all interconnected these days.'

Behind your cone, you smiled. 'I have to say, sir, you're no slouch in a national emergency. The ice cream has saved the day.'

'Miss,' I said, waggling my eyebrows, 'I hope that means you'll allow me to take unspeakable liberties at the first opportunity?'

Your eyes flashed. 'I say' – your accent was perfect – 'steady on.'

That evening, the city came strangely to life. Police patrolled the streets to ward off looters. Paramedics rushed to free people trapped in elevators. Buskers sang hymns. Lovers turned giddy. Old people wept in the dark for the lost and the dead. Teenaged drivers played chicken at the major junctions. Gamblers kept all-night vigils by their slot machines. Surgeons finished operations in the dark. Labouring mothers cried out, not for drugs, but for air conditioning. Undertakers guaranteed embalmed bodies for seven hours, no more. The staff of Big Daddy's Crab Shack bestowed quality frozen shellfish on passers-by. At Florally Yours, prostitutes walked away with wilting bridal bouquets, while, all over Toronto, new life was conjured that night under the forgiving cover of darkness.

The city had a pulse. We could feel it as we walked the streets. Not that we had an alternative. With no back-up generator at our bargain hotel, the electronic room key might as well have been a bloody Boots loyalty card.

The night was sultry. We found that park bench in Bellwoods Park – was that what it was called?

'Look,' you said, and I turned my face skywards. 'You can actually see the stars.'

Then we lay down, pulling each other close to fit, and still we didn't know how dark darkness is.

III. July 2005

This morning, it was only the usual domestic chaos. We'd both overslept. I'd forgotten to switch on the immersion tank, again. I shaved with cold water. You brushed your teeth, crowding me out of the mirror. When you started to floss, I ducked.

'*Ha ha*,' you said. 'Very funny. What do you have on today?'

'A twelfth-century Iranian harpy-shaped cup.'

'What's her problem?'

'Nothing, I hope. The radiography's just come back. I'll check her for cracks or signs of corrosion and go from there.'

'She doesn't know what a lucky harpy she is.'

'That's a harpy for you. Never a word of thanks.'

'I'll ride with you. I'm going to Senate House. My dissertation supervisor has a dentist's appointment or something, so I don't need to meet her now till three.'

'Lovely jubbly . . .' I threw down my razor, pulled on a shirt and grabbed my packed lunch. 'Last one out of here is a rotten harpy!'

You grabbed your rucksack. We passed the cat-lady on the stairs, pungent as ever. Outside we bumped into the postie who stuffed your hand full of mail from Canada. You sifted through it quickly. 'Birthday cards,' you grinned. 'And still three days to go.'

'Show-offs.'

'I'll just drop these back in the flat,' and you were digging for your keys. 'I'll be quick.'

'I was late yesterday, Laura!' I called to your receding back. 'And Monday!'

'I'll be right back!'

I sat down on the steps and counted to ten. Then twenty. Then one hundred and three.

'See?' you said, tripping down the steps. 'You hardly knew I was gone.'

I grabbed your hand. 'Come on.'

'Oh-oh,' you said.

'What now?'

'I forgot to go to the loo.'

'Keep walking,' I said.

'You're not late,' you said.

'I hate rushing,' I said.

'Then let's not.' Your foot was on the step again, but I pulled you back.

The electronic barriers weren't working at Harrow. The queue was slow-moving, restive. From far below, we could hear the hissing of distant brakes. At last we broke through, ran into the blast and squeezed aboard a train as the doors slid shut. The seven fifty-seven had been and gone. This was the nine past eight. Standing room only. Arrive at King's Cross at eight thirty-three. Change to the Piccadilly Line. One stop to Russell Square.

'I'm bursting,' you whispered through the press of bodies.

'Try to think about something else. Look – there's a poem up there. Do you want to meet up for a coffee later?'

'Talk of diuretics isn't helping, Nathan.'

'Yes or no?'

'Um, yes . . .' You were reading the poem overhead.

> The world began with a woman,
> shawl-happed, stooped under a creel,
> whose slow step you recognize
> from troubled dreams . . .

'What time?' I said, reading over your head.

'I don't know . . .'

> . . . You feel
> obliged to help bear her burden

> from hill or kelp-strewn shore,
> but she passes by unseeing
> thirled to her private chore.

You grabbed hold of the pole, steadying yourself as the train pulled into Wembley Park. 'Ten-thirty? Eleven? You say.'

'Ten-thirty? At the tearoom?'

'Of course at the tearoom.' You turned briefly, your face a mock-frown, as if I'd been disloyal. It was an unspoken pact, and I could hear your thoughts, chiding. If I could be casual about our tearoom, might I some day forget our first cup of tea together? If I could forget our first cup of tea, would I also forget the sun and the moon over Bow Hill? And the Bronze Age dead dreaming underground and the nightingale singing? Would I forget the Persian prayer? And Greg's Ice Cream? And the stars teeming over Bellwoods Park?

'That's what I said.' I kissed the top of your head. 'The tearoom at ten-thirty.'

Your smile reappeared. 'Okay.' You glanced at your watch. Eight twenty-two. 'But I'm getting off at King's Cross to find a loo. I'll hop the train after that.'

You leaned into me once more as the carriage swayed into motion. A warm inertia descended on us. It was hard to think about moving from that spot; about our bodies separating in the eventual rush for the platform. Your hair smelled of vanilla. Your bottom nestled in my groin.

Then we were both drawn back into the final stanza of the poem.

> It's not sea birds or peat she's carrying,
> not fleece, nor the herring bright
> but her fear that if ever she put it down
> the world would go out like a light.

★

It did. A hundred feet underground. A white, searing shock, and the bright, ordinary world was extinguished.

'She was going to meet me this morning.' I'm staring at the reference number in my hand. 'There's a tearoom near –'

'Yes,' the WPC says. 'I've noted that.' The line is tinny. In the background, I can hear sharp fragments of many voices. 'But I still need a description. Can you do that for me? Can you describe her, briefly?'

'She's a student . . . Post-grad. She's –'

'White? Black? Asian? Other?'

'White.'

'British?'

'Canadian. But she lives here . . . With me. I mean, we live together.'

'Age?'

'She'll be twenty-eight. In a few days.' You will be.

'Height?'

How can I say I won't have you reduced to your vital statistics? 'Could you possibly just check her name against your lists?'

'I'm afraid there are no lists yet.' I hear a colleague mumble something to her. For a moment I lose her. She returns, distracted. 'Um, maybe there's someone else I can speak to?'

'No . . .' My hands are cold. It's July, for God's sake, but my hands are so cold I can hardly hold the phone.

'Do you know her height, Nathan? Roughly?'

No, I want to tell her, I know your height specifically. 'Five ten and three quarters.'

'So five eleven . . .'

And on your feet, I want to tell this woman. On your sturdy feet.

You're walking.

In a slow, stumbling queue.

Things like this take time.

But I know you, Laura. I know you.

You're on your feet. In that slow-moving press of people.

You're making your way to the surface even now – even *now* – hungry for daylight, for its ordinary blessings.

Sacred Heart

In a lifetime it will beat almost three billion times, yet it is capable of more than twice this. Unravaged, the human heart would beat for two hundred years.

Naomi does not know this. She is nineteen. She knows only that the man beside her on the bench was blue when she turned to him – blue, a colour which up to now was no more than an idea for the sea and the sky. Blue and bloating. A party balloon for a face. An ECG flatline for a mouth. He didn't belong – not there under the horse chestnut outside the High School for Girls. Hadn't she been there every day this week with her lunch, her magazine, and the bench all to herself?

He was already rigid, she explains, when she lifted his hand. Now, he's so stiff they can't unfold his arms to clear the way to his heart, or even lie him flat on the bench because his knees are swollen and locked. He's a human seesaw from an old-fashioned comedy routine, and still, still, they're getting a heartbeat, irregular and remote, unreal as an echo, but a heartbeat none the less. Somewhere in the cold meat-locker of his chest, under the brown tweed jacket and the pullover vest, below the faded shirt he'd buttoned to the neck, he's clamouring for release. A man who looked at her only the once, moving over only slightly, as she sat down with her plastic sandwich box and the women's magazine she's been buying each month to know what it is to feel like a woman. He's in there now running from death, knocking to be let out, to please God be let back into the world again. Only fifty-one, breathes the paramedic, fumbling with a driving licence, but fifty-one seems not unreasonable to her. And the corner of her new bias-cut skirt is wet because something was seeping from him, that's what made her turn, and, in this moment, she can still feel the chill of his hand branded on her palm where she touched him. Even the hairs of his knuckles, starched as they were with the cold of him, go on bristling at her fingertips. And she wants him dead, she wants him still, like she wants old people sexless, so disgusted is she by the force of the human heart.

The smell of him trails her on the hem of her skirt as she walks back to work. Her knees feel like two china plates balanced on a busker's sticks. Her chest flutters. She stops at M&S to collect herself, to feel strong and clean again under the bright, false lights of retail. She has ten minutes. She threads her way through Childrenswear, past Linens and into the decorous calm of Houseware. He'll be on a steel table somewhere by now. Maybe in a cold drawer.

Had she known he wasn't going to move over, she would have found another bench. What kind of a man moves without really moving at all? She'd had no choice but to cross and recross her legs so theirs did not touch. She'd had to balance both her magazine and her lunch on a single knee, with her handbag and her can of fizzy orange on the ground at her feet, so little space had he yielded her. She was wearing shimmer tights. How her legs must have shimmered for him in the bright light of noon.

And when she'd moved her hand to swat away a buzzing of bluebottles, everything had nearly toppled. He would have seen her struggling. Did she hear a choked apology or was it a cough? She'll never know. She remembers only his ankles, and his trousers rolled up in thick, fraying bunches. Here was a man on his own who couldn't shop for himself or sew, a man who knew only what his shaving mirror showed him. And what was that? She can't remember his face, only the pale blue balloon of it knotted at his neck. She struggles for the detail, tries to see again his eyes. Blue or brown? Light or dark? And were they wide or squeezed tight when the pain kicked in the door of his heart? She can't remember, and she can't understand why she can't remember. She'd stared at him, she'd had no choice, flat as he was at last under the paramedics' white paddles. Yet the look of him has vanished into the hazy mirage of her mind, like when Jason went away last summer on the Outward Bound course, only two weeks after they'd started going out, and she'd confessed to Carrie at the salon that she was embarrassed, she felt unfaithful, because she couldn't remember what he looked like. She wanted to picture him, to linger over the thought of him, over his face, his eyes, the dimple in his chin, the funny bit where his beard didn't grow, she really wanted to, but he kept disappearing on her. All she could see was the thick wave of his hair. 'That's why you can't,' said Carrie.

'Why?'

'Because you want to too much.'

Naomi claps her hand over her mouth, but it's too late. The torrent of fizzy drink, egg-and-cress sandwich and low-fat crisps spills into a display vase of imitation lilies. Her eyes stream. The muscles in her calves tremble as if an electric current, and not blood, runs in her veins. Her stomach lurches again. She throws everything up, hollowing herself out.

When she raises her head at last, a child in blue dungarees is staring at her, and the lilies are sprayed with orange. In the near distance, she can hear the quick, castanet click of heels coming close, and she hates him, she hates him, that dead man who would not die, that dead man who would neither let her be nor give her a second thought.

At the salon, she scoops a handful of mints from the bowl by the till and walks, head down, into the tiny staff loo, bolting the door behind her. She shoves all the mints into her mouth at once, chewing them fast, burning her windpipe with their cold fire. She slips off her skirt and runs the stained corner under the hot-water tap, heedless of the dry-cleaning tag. She squeezes it out, then bangs the hand-drier on the wall into motion.

'Naomi, you back? Mrs Deleuze is ready for you at sink 3.'

She drapes the wet skirt over the drier, washes her hands under a scalding tap, digs in her small handbag past the rolled-up magazine, and quickly applies wide strokes of blusher to her bleached cheeks.

'Naomi? You in there?'

She slips into the still damp skirt, unbolts the door, and smiles apologetically at Davina, one of the senior stylists.

Naomi is a hair technician. She will ask Mrs Deleuze if the water temperature is all right. She will remind her to avoid conditioning her crown, as she is prone to an oily build-up at the roots. She will not mention dandruff. Instead, she will recommend tea-tree oil shampoo, essential fatty acids and biotin-rich foods. She will manipulate Mrs Deleuze's scalp as she learned to do on her Indian head-massage training day. She will make pleasant conversation, though she has not had time today to consult Mrs Deleuze's index card. Was her new terrier puppy called Fido or Dido? *Would* Mrs Deleuze name her dog after a pop singer? Naomi thinks not. She will ask after Mrs Deleuze's last holiday, remembering not to mention Mr Deleuze until Mrs Deleuze does so herself. She will not say she found a man, stiff and blue, on the bench beside her at lunch. She will not say, 'Poor man. What a shock for his family. I wonder who he was.' She knows all she needs to know. She knows he was looking at her legs. She knows he was looking at her slim feet in her gold strappy shoes. She knows he sat uncomfortably close. It was awful because Naomi was in the middle of 'Seventeen Ways to Have an Orgasm'.

She's been sleeping with Jason for three months now and is not sure that she's had a proper orgasm yet. That's what she told Carrie one night as they scoured the sinks before closing.

'What do you mean – fuckin' hell, there goes another nail! The glue they give you with these things is cheaper than spit.'

'Like, you know, a *proper* one.'

'Proper? Me, I'm happy with the plain old improper kind any day.' She winked at Naomi, and Naomi laughed, as if she really had got the joke, but the truth was she hadn't, not really, and that was the whole point.

As a child, she had played on the old oak banister that rises from the cellar to the hatch in the floor of her mother's small kitchen. She had tested her own strength, hauling herself up its creaking length by her arms, clutching it with her thighs, as if she was a lone survivor escaping a rising flood. The first time, her legs had fluttered like they'd belonged to someone else, like she was someone else, and she lay still and breathless, under the sound of her mother's light footsteps, her hot cheek pressed to the secret of the banister. But it was different with Jason. Of course it was. Jason was warm and alive. Jason was no piece of dead wood. Jason was everything she wanted. He was handsome. He was strong. How could she become her cellar self in front of Jason? How could she let that happen to her face?

Number 1 – Girl Power. Number 2 – Handiwork. Number 3 – Good Vibrations. Number 4 – Mouth Organ. Number 5 – A Bird in the Hand. Number 6 – G-Spot Magic. Number 7 – Bottoms up! Number 8 – Twist and Shout. Number 9 – Wet Wet Wet. Number 10 – Please Come Again. Today, at lunch, Naomi had only got as far as Number 10 when she noticed the corner of her skirt was damp. Had it rained that morning? Should she have wiped the bench before sitting down?

'Naomi? Naomi, Mrs Deleuze would like a jasmine tea.'

Naomi waits for the kettle to boil. The client in chair 6 is a tall redhead, early thirties. She wants layers after all, and she's telling Zoe, a junior stylist, about the aunt she's just visited in Nice. Naomi has never been to France, not even to the diesel cloud of a French ferry port for a duty-free shopping day.

The redhead is called Claudine. Her family on her mother's side, she explains to Zoe, has had a commercial ice company in Nice since the turn of the century, and the aunt, whom she apparently takes after, was delivering ice one day, back in the fifties, to a famous hotel. 'Picture this,' says Claudine, through a curtain of hair. 'It's a sweltering summer day, in the hundreds, yeah? And my aunt, who's not even eighteen, is waiting in the hotel kitchen for an invoice or something when the phone rings. Someone wants enough crushed ice to fill – wait for it – a *double* bath, and they want it delivered to their room straightaway. The kitchen manager rolls his eyes and says pah! pah! several times. He's understaffed that day as it is, and with the heat and the humidity, the kitchen's an inferno. The last thing anyone wants to do is help some rich bastard to more ice than anyone has a right to. But my aunt, never one to miss an opportunity, gets her pretty backside into gear and delivers not one, not two, but *twelve* tureens of crushed ice to the room all by herself. She knocks once, announces the arrival of the ice through the door, and leaves the trolleys just outside. She's just turning on her heels when . . .'

'When?' Zoe changes her scissors.

Claudine's face peeks through the curtain of red. 'When the door opens and a little dog comes running after her, licking her toes through her sandals and jumping up to say hello. Ten minutes later and guess what?'

'What?' Zoe's cutting hand goes limp.

'My aunt is *in* that double bath with one, a French cabinet minister, two, a toy poodle, and three – no word of a lie – Brigitte Bardot.'

'Never!'

'Swear.'

'But I thought she was an animal activist.'

'How much activity do you want? The worst of it is, when I asked my aunt what happened next, all she would say was, "Zee ice melted, pet."'

Zoe laughs. Davina and Mrs Deleuze, at chair 4, laugh. Naomi does not. She squeezes the jasmine-infusion bag hard. She is glad her aunties do not visit upon her stories of bisexual romps in the bath with house pets. She is glad her aunties live in Streatham.

Tonight, even though it's Friday, and balmy too, she and Jason will not have sex in his little brother's pop-up garden tent because his coach says he's got to save it for the away game tomorrow. But he will kiss her a long goodnight among the KitKat and Galaxy bar boxes in the alleyway between the One-Stop and her mother's house. He will press himself, hard against her. He will show her again, on his special sports performance watch, how she makes his digital heart rate race. And she will leave him, unsure why she didn't mention, even once, the man on the bench.

All night she is restless. She tells herself it's the mobile phone under her pillow. Jason is going to ring her first thing from the team mini-bus and she cannot miss his call. He needs her to say, in a voice just for him, 'Go get 'em, Lightning Man,' the way Posh might say it to Becks. It's his lucky saying, and his private name for his thingy, the one she sometimes whispers in his ear when she nuzzles him. She can't remember how it started or where it came from but now, come what may, she has to whisper it to him before each game, even though she is in fact too embarrassed to ever say it with the throaty desire he would, on these occasions, like. It's the only thing Jason is irrational about so she tries to oblige as best she can, like when he wants her to go down on him and the force of him at the back of her throat almost makes her dinner come up, but she keeps at it anyway, and swallows too, even though the thick salty slick of it makes her stomach judder, even though Carrie's told her there are over a thousand calories in every ejaculation, and Naomi wonders if that's why she's putting on weight, like the prostitute Carrie read about – the one who ate nothing, smoked fags instead, but swallowed several times a day and put on three stone. Naomi does it anyway since what kind of girl would tell her boyfriend she can't because she might throw up all over his thingy. His bit of lightning in this world.

Still, when the call comes, she jumps from sleep, her heart banging like an old tin can tied to a bumper.

Incoming call. Not Jason. Not Carrie either. 'Hello?'

'Miss Naomi Phillips?' A woman's voice.

'Yes.' Naomi crosses her legs and pulls her duvet around her.

'This is the Patient Care Office at St Richard's. I believe you passed your details to one of our paramedic teams yesterday.'

Naomi almost hits the call-ended button. She wants to say, this is a mistake. If she'd known he was going to die, she wouldn't have sat down in the first place.

'Yes. They asked me to fill out a form.'

Already, in her mind, she is rehearsing the words: she will not be able to attend the funeral, she is glad she was able to do what little she could.

'We thought we'd update you on Mr Peter Bartholomew.'

It is a long moment before Naomi realizes that the woman on the phone is talking about the man on the bench. She doesn't like him having a name. She can't quite believe he has – had – a name.

'I'm pleased to tell you he survived surgery.'

What surgery? Naomi's chest goes hollow, as if something has punctured her lungs. 'But the man I saw was –'

'It's only natural you feared the worst.'

'He wasn't –'

'An understandable mistake. That's why I wanted to –'

' – breathing.'

'Yesterday must have been very upsetting for you, Miss Phillips. That's why I'm glad to be able to give you some good news. Mr Bartholomew's condition is clearly critical, and I cannot over-emphasize the seriousness of the situation, but –'

'There's still hope.' Naomi's legs go numb below her. Suddenly she feels half dead herself.

'Since the operation, Mr Bartholomew has been in and out of consciousness. All we can say at this point is, that's encouraging.'

'Yes.'

'He has said very little. However, one of our staff nurses told him he was a lucky man, that a young woman phoned 999 on her mobile phone. He seemed to become a little more coherent. The nurse had the impression he'd like to thank you. That's nice, isn't it? Nice to know you made a difference.'

'There's no need. I only –'

'Visiting time is strictly limited in the cardio unit, and usually only family, but under the circumstances, and given that there seems to be no one else, we felt it right to let you know.'

'Of course I'd like to come, but I'm on lates this week. I'm a hair technician. My shifts don't start till three-thirty so that means I'm on late every night this week.'

'We generally discourage evening visits in the cardio unit. Come any time between twelve and four. I'll register your name at the reception desk. You can tell them you spoke to Mrs Booth.'

Naomi gets up and locks her bedroom door. She doesn't want her mother to come in. She has to think. How is he doing this to her? How is he stitching her life to his even still? How has he twisted everything around? Blue but still breathing. Helpless but demanding. Passive but rigid as a corpse.

When Jason rings, Naomi panics. He tells her they're almost at Grantham, that the pitch is supposed to be rubbish, it's raining there, and if she's wondering what the stink is, it's Jimmy's kit, and she should close her bedroom window. There's a battery of laughter, and he says low, just for her, that he thought he'd give her a quick call. He wanted to hear her voice.

Her cue.

'Naomi, you there?'

'Yes. And – I wanted to tell you something.'

'What's that then?' His voice is warm as beer. He tells her to wait. He moves to an empty seat at the back of the bus. They go through a tunnel and lose each other.

'Naomi?'

'Still here.'

'I'm listening.'

'There's someone else, Jason.' She doesn't know what she means. But she says it again. 'I'm really sorry, Jason. There's someone else.'

Down corridor after corridor, through Witterings Ward, Middleton, and back again. She can't concentrate. Many-eyed machines on wheels, on two legs, on leads, litter her route like a strange, watchful menagerie. She doesn't belong here. She is a fraud. The seedless grapes in her hand are from her mother's fridge. She cannot even remember what the man on the bench looks like. Outside a patients' toilet, a nurse is laughing with a one-legged man. 'See, Harold? What did I tell you? Your sins will find you out.'

On her left, she passes a door marked DIRTY UTILITY ROOM. 'Please keep this door shut.' But it's not. Naomi sees a wide sink, a black bin for waste labelled INCINERATE ONLY, and a stack of commodes under another sign: IF YOU RETURN IT, YOU WASH IT.

Down the corridor, two giggling cleaning girls in fitted green smocks, sunbed tans and platform shoes wrap themselves in cellophane aprons and gloves they pull from a dispenser on the wall. She wonders what might splash on them; where they will have to put their hands. She wonders if they have read the notice on the wall about the proper way for staff to wash their hands. 'Do not forget your thumb,' the final line warns, and Naomi suddenly feels she is wandering alone in a world where danger is at your fingertips.

At the cardio reception desk, the nurse ticks her name off a list, confiscates the grapes like she would a petty weapon, ushers her into a ward and pulls back a plastic curtain to reveal what Naomi assumes must be the man from the bench. She does as the nurse says and pulls a chair up to the foot of the bed. His eyes are closed. She does not know if he is asleep or unconscious. She does not ask. She tries to summon the face under the bubble of the mask, but it's lost in the mist of his ventilated breath.

She looks around, nervously. Eight beds. Six men. Windows too high and narrow to see through if you're confined to a bed. Two other visitors, both women. At the end of the ward, one, middle-aged, with a face like porridge that has set in the pan. Across from Naomi, another, old but dignified. A Chichester lady. A major's wife, Naomi decides. Her lipstick is well applied. She has a clear widow's peak, which must have been striking when she was younger – Naomi would tell her as much if the major's wife were a client at the salon. She would not say that, the truth is, she can never really imagine old people any younger than they are.

Technology pulses and sighs. Here, in the dim hush of this place, drips, defibrillators, ventilators, pacemakers, balloon pumps and Hewlett-Packard monitors are more alive than the anonymous hearts and lungs over which they watch. It scares her. She wonders how long she has to stay. She doesn't feel right sitting beside the still body of a strange man, possibly naked except for the cheap, hospital-issue blanket over him. What does the major's wife imagine? she wonders.

She crosses her legs and her left foot accidentally kicks the end of the bed. Its metal frame shudders. 'Sorry,' she whispers. To bed or man, she is not sure. She stands, walks to the window behind his bed, and pretends to take in the view. The back wall of the hospital laundry. Mounds of linen in rolling skips glide in and out of double doors. She almost took a job as a chambermaid once, the summer before her GCSEs, but the thought of the sheets of strangers made her turn to Shippams and fish paste instead.

Rain spits at the window. She turns. Finds herself suddenly near him – over him. They've shaved his chest. The light is poor but if she squints she can see the new growth of dark stubble rising below the pale, flaccid skin. He is pierced all over like that saint in the picture she saw on a school trip to the National Gallery, the one with the long hairless body and all those arrows sticking out of his white, white flesh. There's a needle in his chest, his arm, his wrist, his hand. Twisty tubing springs from each, like the plastic crazy straws her mother used to buy to get Naomi to drink her milk. For a time, she cannot stop herself watching the slow drip of his wound into the drain-bag at the side of the bed. She does not know a word for the colour.

Beyond the wound, through the tubing and wires, there are red electrodes taped like too many nipples to his sunken chest. He doesn't look real somehow. She stares at his chest, and for a moment it seems as if she need only take the blue biro out of her bag and connect the dots to bring him back into being.

She takes her seat once more and resumes her role as a visitor. 'Hello,' she tries in a low voice. 'Hello?' Miracles are possible. This is the Church of the Heart. 'I'm Naomi. I'm the girl who phoned for an ambulance. I think you wanted to see me?'

The IV monitor starts to bleep angrily. Naomi sits back, embarrassed. The nurse who seized her grapes arrives, pushes past her chair, adjusts a dial, and fingers the drip-feed suspiciously. 'You haven't touched this?' Across the room, the major's wife looks up.

Naomi shakes her head, eyes wide. Do they think she wants him in pain? Do they think she wants to kill him? Will this nurse demand to know her exact relationship to the man from the bench?

'Been playing up all week,' she sighs. 'Must be faulty. I'll order a replacement, okay?'

'Thank you,' says Naomi, relieved, relieved not to stand

accused, relieved that the nurse feels instead she must be account-able to her. Naomi is important. Suddenly she is the loved one of the mortally wounded. The nurse smiles at her briefly and leaves.

Naomi tries again, quietly, so the major's wife can't hear. 'Perhaps you don't remember me. I'm Naomi. I'm nineteen. I live here in Chichester. I'm a hair technician. I was having lunch on the same bench as you just yesterday. There were all those flies buzzing round, remember? Weren't they a nuisance? And I was reading a magazine. Of course you might not have noticed me. I was wearing, um, gold sandals. Anyway, that was me. I mean, um, those were my feet.'

'I SAY, IS THIS A CHINESE SEX OUTFIT?'

Naomi swivels in her chair. The major has sat up and is shouting from his bed. 'IS THIS A CHINESE SEX OUTFIT?'

The major's wife tries to shush him into submission. She pats his hand. She wipes his bald head with a damp cloth.

'IS THIS OR IS THIS NOT A CHINESE SEX OUTFIT?'

Her coiffed silver hair slips loose, falling over her face, into her mouth. 'The morphine,' she apologizes to Naomi from across the room. 'And the cataracts don't help, I'm afraid.'

Naomi smiles kindly, one wife to another. It gives her courage. She stands, picks up her chair, and moves it from the foot of the bed to the side. She bends down and opens the small plyboard cupboard squeezed awkwardly between the bed and the IV monitor. His clothes. The ones he was admitted in. One by one, she refolds them: the brown tweed jacket; the pullover vest; the faded cotton shirt, its buttons ripped off in the scrabble for his heart; the trousers with the frayed hems; a pair of white briefs; brown socks; black shoes with worn laces. She returns each item to the cupboard with care. Then she takes the hand of the man from the bench in hers.

She sits by his side for two and a half hours. She sits until ten past three when she has to leave at last for her shift at the salon. He does not open his eyes even once. He does not squeeze her hand.

'Tomorrow,' says the nurse. 'Try again tomorrow. I had a few good minutes with him this morning, you know. It's just going to take time.' And she returns Naomi's mother's grapes to her.

The following morning, she wakes to the sound of voices downstairs. Her mother and – she listens – Jason.

She takes her time. She irons her hair so it falls sleekly past her shoulders. She slips into a clingy pink summer dress with spaghetti straps. Her nipples rise through the jersey. Which is fine. Nipples are in. Nipples are the new cleavage. She finds one gold sandal under the bed and the other in the wardrobe. She squirts her wrists and neck with Elizabeth Arden eau de toilette. She reaches for a delicate white cardigan that ties at the breast with a single silk ribbon.

The clack of her sandals on the stairs is unabashed.

'Naomi, I was just going to wake you. Jason's here. To help us clean out the cellar, like he said last week. Isn't that nice? He thinks he might even be able to replace that rickety old banister. I'm sure it's got woodworm.'

Jason smiles nervously. 'You look lovely.'

Her mother has made him a cup of tea. She will have remembered that he likes two sugars and lots of milk. Her mother likes Jason. Too much. 'If I were twenty years younger,' she had teased him once.

Now she's giving him a conspiratorial smile. 'I'll get back to "Woman's Hour" then.' He has told her. That Naomi has someone else. That her only daughter is leading a double life. She cannot believe it will last. She cannot believe a daughter of hers will pass up a boy like Jason.

'I'm on my way out, Mum.'

'But the cellar.'

'Can't today. Sorry.'

'I thought you were on lates this week. That's why I asked Jason round this morning.'

'I'll give you a ring later. Bye, Jason.'

'I'll walk you into town.'

'No. Finish your tea. I'm fine.'

Her mother's house smells of pot pourri. Outside, the breezy sunshine is a relief. She fills her lungs. Her heart quickens. Women, Jason once said, have faster heart rates than men. Today, she feels this must be true. She has life enough to share.

She hardly looks up as she walks. She wonders what colour his eyes will be when they open. She wonders that the most.

When the double doors of the hospital slide back she realizes she is early. Visiting hours don't start for another forty minutes. The hospital shop is open. She looks at the cards, but decides against one. Get Well Soon cards are from acquaintances. She chooses instead a sewing kit, a comb, a nail clipper, some lotion for extra-dry skin, a pack of disposable razors and a magazine for ramblers. 'He loves walking in the Downs,' she hears herself telling the major's wife.

When she arrives at the desk, the same nurse looks up. Naomi smiles, juggling her purchases.

'I'm very sorry. You can't go in.'

'Sorry, I'm early, aren't I? I thought maybe –'

'Miss Phillips, is it?'

'Yes, my name's on your list? I was here yesterday?' Her voice does this sometimes – turns statements into questions. Someone asked her once if she was Australian.

'I'm very sorry, Miss Phillips. Mr Bartholomew passed away this morning.'

'He passed a what?'

'He passed away. I'm so sorry. Please, sit down. Let me take your things.'

'But just yesterday, you said he –'

'He was critical. Let me get you a glass of water. It's a shock, I know it is.'

She hates this nurse. She hated her yesterday by the IV drip. She hated her too for her 'few good minutes' with the man from the bench. 'He can't be. Perhaps you've got the wrong bed. He was in the one by the door –'

'It was heart failure. I'm afraid our efforts at resuscitation failed. The doctors did everything they could. Would you like to speak to one of the team? Would you like a doctor to explain?'

'No.' She has read the poster. It hangs outside the door of the ward. She can see it now over the nurse's blue shoulder. She doesn't know why medical staff need a poster to tell them about cardiac life support. 1: Mouth-to-mouth ventilation. 2: Administer precordial thump. 3: Place paddles correctly. 4: Give oxygen. 5: Intubate. 6: Cannulate large vein.

'Can I ring someone for you? A taxi perhaps? A friend? We have a chaplain on staff.'

'Can I see him? Mr Bartholomew, I mean. Is he here still?'

'Let's give it some thought. Why don't you sit down?'

'I want to see him.'

'The fact is, the porters will be here shortly.' She pauses, studies the blank insistence of Naomi's face. 'Okay. Take a few minutes. Slip through the curtains.'

The hospital-issue blanket is gone. He's almost unchanged against the fresh white sheets. Paler. But better in some way. No mask, needles, tubes or wires. She can see the outline of his thighs through the single sheet that covers him. More muscular than she would have thought. 'He loved walking in the Downs.' Will she be able to tell the major's wife?

His hands are by his sides, bloodied slightly where the needles for the drips have been withdrawn. The wounds are small stigmata, like the ones she saw in that documentary the other night about the supernatural.

He will not bleed for her.

Someone has left a piece of transparent surgical tape on one wrist. There's another strip on his chest. She moves to his side, hesitates, then peels each piece away. The skin hardly lifts with it. She raises his hand, his arm. He's stiff. Cold.

Again.

Beneath her white cardigan, beneath her pink summer dress, Naomi's heart clenches into a raw fist.

Later, she will not remember slipping off her sandals. She will not remember climbing on to the bed. She'll remember only the sharp stillness of the ward, the sweat at the back of her knees, and the explosion of words in her mouth as she rode the dead muscle of his thigh.

Love me. Love me.

Live Wire

You used to say you knew I was in a room before you saw me; that the air smelled like it did after a rainfall. Ionized.

Energy is eternal delight. I read that once, but I knew it when I was a child, shuffling my way in sock-feet over the creamy shag carpet, charging myself. 'Oh! You've given me a shock,' my mother's elbow would cry, wrinkled and vulnerable at the edge of the kitchen table. I can see the scene again. Behind my mother's back, a smile gets the better of my babyface, and I shuffle my way back through the living room, where our ancient beagle lazes like a fitful lung under the big bay window. Outside, the black cables of power lines are swaying against a purple, rain-bloated sky. The soles of my feet are tingling with static, my toes are curling with it, and I'm stretching out my index finger. My mood-ring from the cereal box flashes blue when I make contact with the tip of Brutus's sleeping tail. I see it twitch with the secret current of me.

Remember the Powergen woman who came on before the late-night weather? 'Powergen,' she pronounced in her smoky voice. 'Generating electricity whatever the weather.' She arose in black latex from a storm cloud of open umbrellas. A plume of water rose impossibly from her head, teasing the eye. Her face was white, her pupils were huge, and she was unapologetically fatal.

That first time, I called you Dr Numb. I wanted to shock you. As the nurse wheeled in the electroencephalograph, I asked if you had ever wanted to have your way with a woman once you'd put her under. My eyebrows flickered, but you remained composed. Don't be shy, I said – *ether* you have or you haven't – and your eyes smiled above your green mask.

The gag tasted of peppermint. My earrings were removed, then my shoes. As I raised my head to check the state of my socks, a bright needle rose on the horizon. Muscle relaxant, the nurse smiled, so you don't do yourself an injury. I'm relaxed, I mumbled through the gag. You won't be with a bone fracture, she chuckled. Then the dials were spinning, the flowmeters were at high tide, and you were lowering the mask and hose on to my face, brushing a wisp of hair from my cheek. In no time I was inhaling the sweet smell of halothane and rising, over the song of the electrocardiogram, over you, over the balding head of Dr Burns, and slipping into the earth's upper atmosphere as if I were moving through water. Far below me, electrical storms were raging in the darkness, and in that upside-down, head-over-heels world, I was the golden key on the kite. The fuse of bright hair in the candle flame. The live wire. The finger of Adam. The spark in the synapse. You stood and watched seventy volts of electricity enter me, and in that moment, you wanted to enter me too.

I remember that, as I was coming to in the recovery room, you risked a breach of professional conduct. So how was that – for you – Gloria? you said, lurching into comedy, and as you did so, your throat blushed. You regretted the question the moment it escaped your mask. My mouth and jaw were slack with the anaesthetic. My head was humming like a plucked harp string. I felt nauseous. But you were grateful for my lopsided smile.

On our first date, you were frightened someone would see you with me. We sat in a hospital bus shelter with two cups of takeaway coffee. From where we sat, we could see the smoke-stack of the hospital incinerator; what once had been blood and bone climbed high into the atmosphere. We talked mostly about the weather: recent droughts, hosepipe bans, the greenhouse effect, El Niño. I said, the snowdrops are already up, it gets earlier every year, and you nodded. I breathed in tendrils of steam. You said it looked like rain. I said, have you ever been in the hospital mortuary? and your coffee sloshed over the side of your cup, burning your hand. I smiled nervously, trying to say, can we pretend I didn't say that? Why on earth did I say that? Then: yes, you said, as a student, years ago. And since then? I heard myself asking. Once, only the once. I nodded. You sipped the remains of your coffee. I played with a hangnail. Did you see anyone – any body, I mean? A middle-aged man, you said. And did you look at him? No, you hadn't, there was no reason to, but the coroner had shown you the bruising from the blow he'd sustained to the back of his skull. He'd been hit? I said. Yes – and you turned to look at me – by a hailstone.

Talk of the weather became our private language, a code for intimacy and evasion. On our second date, after a particularly rich meal in a tiny Italian restaurant, I inquired indelicately about winds from the torrid zone. You blushed brightly, answering with an embarrassed nod as the waiter poured the espresso, quickly. After an evening of malt whisky from the bottle behind the books in your office, I tapped your groin and asked for the forecast. A low-pressure system is sadly upon us, you reported, and I laughed. I sweet-talked you with murmurings of cold snaps and warm spells. I coaxed you with word of lunar eclipses and vernal equinoxes. We walked everywhere in all weather, dodging imaginary hailstones, goading death.

I can't remember when you started reading: weather reports, shipping forecasts, farmers' almanacs, compendiums of freak-weather occurrences. But one day, you tried to describe for me the mystery at the eye of a tornado, and I remember your pupils, vast as you looked at me. I said I loved high winds, whirlwind courtships, and windy nights for lovemaking; I liked the rattling of the window-panes because the whole world seemed to be shaking with you. You said, did I know? women were more likely to conceive in July and December, when the magnetic fields associated with solar winds are low. I declared myself a slave to the elements, and especially to magnetic fields. An electro-magnetic personality, that's me, I sang, and your eyes narrowed. I couldn't tell what you were thinking.

Once, you showed me a picture in a library book of a woman disfigured by lightning. I traced the red scar tissue on her chest with my finger. It's beautiful, I said; it's like an oak tree spring-ing from her breastbone, see? And suddenly you saw it too. I told you about the hot dry winds of the world: the Fohn off the Alps, the Mistral in southern France, the Chinook on the prairies of Canada, the Sirocco that blows out of North Africa. All famous for inducing madness. You said, thank goodness we can rely on the good old British damp. Can we? I said, and I blew in your ear. Warm dry winds, I whispered, blow down from the Cotswolds, disquieting the citizens of Cheltenham, and winds, hot as stale breath, creep down from the Pennines and rub the stubborn necks of Yorkshiremen, predisposing even them to dreams and whimsy. You're joking, you said. Yes, I am, and I paused. It's actually much worse than that, the madness. Be serious, you said. I *am* being serious. And you were quiet for the rest of the day.

Sometimes, in your bed, we'd talk dreamily about buying a satellite dish so we could sleep to the blue flicker of the twenty-four-hour weather channel. We slept with the window open because I loved the smell of the night. Once, we heard a fox barking by the rubbish skip behind your building, and the smell of it – a whiff of damp fur and stale earth – climbed up through the window and between the cotton sheets. You said you couldn't smell it for the smell of my skin and you inhaled me like an irresistible stimulant, pushing your nose between my breasts, down my belly and over the rounds of my thighs. Sometimes, as we made love and you yearned within me, I knew you'd bury yourself in me if you could, that you'd rest there like a baby, or a body, your ear tuned to the blood frequency of my heart.

Then sleep: sometimes, your groin a pillow for my head, your cock soft by my cheek like a thumb that had slipped from my mouth, and your legs around my legs; two strong roots earthing me.

You never asked what was wrong with me, though you were there, administering my halothane breeze at ninety, one hundred, and one hundred and ten volts. Two sessions per week. Four weeks of treatment. Perhaps you had seen the case notes. You would have assumed mania. I spoke too fast, thought too fast, slept too little, sensed too much and I craved a life for ever in the moment as much as you craved the ephemera of the past.

You're mad, I said, when I discovered your stash of weekly checklists in a desk drawer: yellowed scraps of paper with references to your ex-wife's dental appointments; to a deposit for a Greek holiday taken last year; to a pair of shoes that had long since been repaired. It was your weakness, you confessed; a kind of superstition. Relics of the past – inconsequential things in themselves – reminded you you were alive.

As a child, you had chalked your name on city walls. You'd scratched I WAS HERE on wooden desks with the tip of your schoolboy compass. You had ticket stubs from 1972; a bracelet your first girlfriend had left behind in your mother's house; a novel you reread once every year. You wanted a song we could call ours. 'Crazy', I suggested, but I could tell from the look on your face you weren't confident the joke was on me. You wanted places to remember us by; favourite haunts; anniversaries; a string of photo-booth snaps to discover weeks later in your coat pocket. You wanted the ghost of my voice on your answering-machine; strands of my hair on your sheets.

I wanted the smell of you in my nostrils; your lips on mine in the ladies' toilets; the ricochet of our words in an argument; the shy surprise of your laughter; the two of us counting backwards together before the big blue zing; the pulse in my clitoris at the thought of you. I wanted to bring you to life. Over and over.

Insatiable, you called me by night.

Oh, my dear one, I'd whisper back. Oh, my own sweet deadbeat. Rise again, rise again.

There is a saying among maniacs: a hundred and thirty volts for quick canonization. I said, imagine my entry in *Lives of the Saints*. 'Saint Gloria, Ecstatic (1969–99): martyred at the switch-happy hands of Dr Burns, consultant psychiatrist. *In excelsis Glo-ri-a*.' Think of the radiance, I said. Think of the glow.

It was the eve of my final treatment. The voltage was to be increased again. Dr Burns had yet to find my seizure threshold.

We'd had a late dinner. We were waiting for the late-night weather. You were washing up. I was leafing through one of your medical journals.

What does 'awareness' mean?

You looked up over the sink of dishes.

I read aloud: 'Experimentation must be cautious, at best, if complications such as awareness are to be avoided.'

It's just a complication.

I know that. It says that. Why don't you ever want to talk about work?

I don't *not* want to talk about work.

Well, now's your chance.

Okay. During anaesthetic paralysis, the patient receives what we call intermittent positive pressure ventilation, or IPPV. If sufficient anaesthesia isn't maintained at that stage, it's possible for him or her to be completely conscious, in terrible pain, and totally incapable of movement or speech. It's a nightmare situation, worthy of Poe, but in the tradition of medical understatement we simply call it 'awareness'.

Could be the dream cure this mad woman's been looking for.
That's why I don't talk about the hospital.

You don't like it when I refer to my condition.

I don't like it when you talk nonsense.

That's what mad people do.

You're not 'mad'.

Could you maybe mention it to Dr Burns tomorrow before he throws the switch?

It's not electrocution we're talking about, and you know his name isn't Dr Burns.

I bet you love it when I shake.

You haven't yet, Gloria. That's the problem.

The weather was on. My back was to you, and I was crying. You dried your hands, got hold of the control and turned up the volume. You said I should calm down, make it an early night, have a glass of wine from the bottle of red we'd opened at dinner. You gave me a glass from the drainer, still hot to the touch. The Powergen woman had appeared atop her storm cloud of black umbrellas. I remember her strange smile and the syncopated sound of falling rain, like an erratic pulse on an ECG. You straightened up from pouring the wine, wondered fleetingly where you'd left the cork, passed me the glass, then returned to a corner of the kitchen and picked up the control again. When you turned to me, your face was a question mark with no mask to hide it, for the glass in my hand was flying through the air, tangential as a hailstone.

Shards of claret rained down. I was seeing red, and red was gushing from your temple.

For Christ's sake, Gloria!

Mad yet? I shouted. Because I certainly am! Tell Dr Burns to wire up the cowstunner!

Gloria! Calm down!

I was at your bedroom window and shouting on to the street: Do you hear that, you residential respectables? You bunch of human speed bumps! Well, restrain me, Doctor, why don't you! Go on. Then fuck me! Fuck me like you've been doing from the start!

I did for you what you couldn't do for yourself, slowly and by degree that night. I let you let go of your uneasy effort at life. I opened your desk drawer and tossed your horde of checklists out of the window into the street beyond. I reached into your bedroom cupboard for your shoe box of newspaper cuttings, old photos and souvenirs, and I pitched it on to the rubbish skip where that fox had once lingered. I filled your quiet, ordinary street with a maniac's protests and laughter. That night, for the first time, you felt too much. Insufficient anaesthesia. Awareness.

Later, in bed, I pulled you out of your sleep, exhausted, and on to me – a dead weight on my thumping heart.

Then they were wheeling me out of the prep room, past the long ward that smelled of the sweet rot of old flowers, down a ramp, past the mortuary with the insect-stunners on the ceiling, through the pain clinic, and into the treatment room for the final time. I saw the back of you at the anaesthesia machine. On my other side, a nurse I hadn't seen before was bent over a tray, untangling the delicate filaments of the electrodes. They reminded me of the Crazy String I'd once sprayed over Brutus and all the trees in our garden.

The doctor is here, the nurse said automatically, so not to worry.

Call me delusional, I said, but I can't see him.

That's because he's instructing a group of students, behind the two-way mirror over there.

All seeing, I quipped.

Hmmm?

Like God. It was just a joke.

If I'm not mistaken, she bristled, there's a two-way mirror at the back of the Our Price shop on the high street.

I turned my head to where you stood. You were confirming the colour coordinates on the anaesthesia tubing with a second nurse. Halo-thane, here I come, I said.

You turned around and it wasn't you. It wasn't you.

Somebody wheeled in an IV drip. I was speaking to the likeness of you, a man in green surgical gear and a mask, and suddenly I couldn't remember the colour of your eyes. I never have the intravenous, I tried to explain. I always go under with the mask. (Your hand at my face. The two of us counting backwards. The sweet, sultry breeze in my head.)

The drip is easier, he was telling me. You're less likely to get excited.

Excited? Excited how?

It's just what we call it. As you lose consciousness, your body might well resist. You might cough or vomit. Your feet might kick the air. Some patients hold their breath, like children trying to turn themselves blue. It rarely happens with the IV induction. It's easier on you.

I *always* go under with the mask. Ask your colleague, Doctor . . . Doctor . . . Your surname was gone from my mind. Is he back there, behind the glass?

A door opened in the mirror and Dr Burns appeared: No, I'm afraid he's unable to assist today. However, if you prefer the inhalational induction, Gloria, I'm sure –

Something's happened to him. Otherwise he'd be here.

I saw the nurse with the electrodes and the second nurse exchange a look. Dr Burns asked if I'd been given a pre-med.

She doesn't usually need one, someone answered.

I have to go to the mortuary, I said.

The mortuary?

I have to go.

We'll take you back to the prep room, Gloria, give you a sedative, and see how you feel after that.

I can't go anywhere until I've been to the mortuary.

I sat up on the table, swung my sock-feet over the side, and slipped as they hit the polished floor. Then someone was at either elbow and the nurse with the electrodes was saying poor thing, and I knew I'd never be ecstatic again.

He's dead, I said quietly. Dr Numb is dead.

Listen to me, Gloria. We're taking you back to the prep room. We'll talk things over there.

I remember a hushing of voices like white noise in my ear, and a yellow tablet on my tongue.

When I came to, you were at the edge of my bed, ashen-faced. The gash on your forehead had drawn all the colour from your cheeks. I said, I tried to go to you in the mortuary. They wouldn't let me go.

I know, you said.

The cut . . .

I can't feel it any more.

How did it all happen?

I'm not sure.

I mortified you, didn't I?

Never mind now.

Have there been complaints?

Some. A couple of notes through my door.

And here, in the hospital?

There might be disciplinary procedures. It doesn't matter.

Because you can't feel anything. Because I mortified you.

I have to go now, Gloria.

I sat up, circled your waist with my arms, and pressed my streaming face into your chest. Your back was rigid. Your hand, when it finally touched my head, was cold.

They're going to try me on the lithium again, I said.

It won't be too bad.

No Saint Gloria.

No.

I inhaled the familiar smell of your shirt. What will I do now that you're gone?

You'll be okay.

Will I? And what about you?

I'll live.

I smiled. It was your first breezy joke.

I love you, Dr Numb.

I love you too, Gloria.

I could feel you leaving me. Suddenly, everything was urgent, and I was speaking through your shirt, into your chest, into the cold, frightened heart of you: I can't bring you back. Do you understand? I can't bring you back, but I can't be your grave either.

Through the narrow window in the prep-room door, I watched two porters pass at speed with a stretcher between them. The air is so heavy, I said. Do you find the air heavy?

Sleep now, you said.

E-Love: Heloise & Abelard

Extant Instant Messages

Heloise: Further intercourse?!

Abelard: Write anything, even a couple of words if u can. A gift for letters is so rare in women! xxx

Heloise: If that is an invitation to disputation, it has missed its mark.

Abelard: ;–)) Have mercy on your beloved, wasting away.

Heloise: How you talk! You are stronger than steel. Although it may be in the future, I already see the mountaintops bowing down before you.

Abelard: What else does the prophet foretell? ;–))

Heloise: I would write more but few words instruct a wise man.

Abelard: Indeed your words are few but I have made them many by rereading them. And I am never far from the knowledge of you: how fertile with delight is your breast, how you shine with pure beauty. Body so full of moisture – that indescribable scent of yours . . . Even if I could write to you continuously so that I did nothing else, your merits are so many that I could not count them all.

Heloise: And you, you are sweeter from day to day, and loved now as much as possible and always loved more than anything.

Abelard: Ask what I did after I wrote last time.

Heloise: ???

Abelard: I threw myself on to the bed out of impatience. ;-))

Heloise: And me, unjustly deprived!

Abelard: You are inside my breast for ever. You are with me until I fall asleep. You never leave me, and when I wake I see you before even the light of day.

Heloise: Know indeed that the midday sun has risen for you. And look too how, now that this slight snow has melted, all things flourish again.

Abelard: My brightest star (whose rays I have recently enjoyed!), may I gaze endlessly at you alone, ignoring the light of day.

Heloise: Such talk. Yet no phrase has yet been found that speaks clearly about how intent on you is my spirit. For God is my witness that I love you, Peter Abelard, with a sublime and exceptional love. And so there is not nor ever will be any event or circumstance, except only death, that will separate me from your love.

Abelard: I could not bear it, truly. Physicists say often that the moon does not shine without the sun, and that when deprived of this light, it is robbed of all benefit of heat and brightness and presents to humans a dark ashen sphere . . .

Heloise: Then I give you the most precious thing I have – myself, firm in faith and love, steady in desire, never changeable. There is no one in this world breathing life–giving air whom I desire to love more than you. Indeed, what need is there even for words?

Abelard: None. Now that our love has grown so strong that it shines forth by itself, there is little need of words because we are overflowing with what is real. Farewell then – from the friend who has always been, he who sends you the same constancy of love.

Heloise: Farewell? Already? Friend?!!!

Abelard: Problem?

. . .

Abelard: Ellie? :–((

Heloise: What say your other friends when you kiss their breasts?

Abelard: ?**!

Heloise: From now on, may all our writing cease.

Abelard: I do not know what so great sin of mine preceded that in such a short space you could wish to throw away completely all feelings of compassion and intimacy for me!

Heloise: And you famed for your logic!

. . .

Abelard: Ellie?

. . .

Abelard: Ellie . . . U there?

Heloise: Do not dissemble. I think you are not unaware that ashes placed on a sleeping fire never put it out.

Abelard: Forgive me my ashen ways. Instruct me.

Heloise: You desire it?

Abelard: Truly.

Heloise: My case is this.

Abelard: And I will not dispute it.

Abelard: Go gently though.

Abelard: That is to say, have mercy.

Heloise: Surely in you I have discovered the greatest and most outstanding good of all.

Abelard: You make a poor case. I am guilty, I who compelled you to sin.

Heloise: **Desist!**

Abelard: **Apologia.**

Heloise: I repeat: Surely in you I have discovered the greatest and most outstanding good of all. *And*, since it is established that your goodness is eternal, it is for me the proof beyond doubt that you will remain in my love for eternity.

*

Heloise: What are u saying?! Intent – that is to say, true feeling – is all we have. Virtue is a whore beside it. She cares for appearances only. Did you not teach me as much?

Abelard: I say only that it is not unreasonable if sometimes – now, for example – we alternate between visiting each other and writing when we cannot.

Heloise: U tire of me.

Abelard: I do not tire of u. I say only that it is not unreasonable.

Heloise: Reason best serves truth. Why do you now apprentice it to falsehood? Tell me what I have done. Forgive me it.

Abelard: I would forgive you readily, most beloved, even if you had committed some serious act against me, because too hard would he be whom your speech so tender and amiable could not soften. But truly you have no need of forgiveness, because you have not wronged me in any way.

Heloise: **Then it is as I feared. U tire of me.**

Abelard: **No.**

Heloise: **Yet you are not direct. You are not yourself.**

Abelard: **U worry 2 much**

Heloise: **And if u are not urself, if ur heart no longer speaks to mine, everything is lost.**

Abelard: **I say only that the written word serves us better than most.**

Heloise: **That is not all you say. How u dissemble. How u change.**

Abelard: **And how u milk my words.**

Heloise: **It is the words u don't write. In them, I read what I already feared: if your love is lost, all that is left us is suffering as great as our love has been.**

Abelard: **No more prophesying, I beg you.**

Heloise: **The present is challenge enough. Of course I know that where there is passion and love there is always struggle and turmoil. Yet I know too that now I am tired. I can no longer reply to you because you are taking sweet things as burdensome and, in doing so, you sadden my spirit.**

Abelard: **There is no burden. It is as I say. I have spoken to my sister in Brittany. She will care for the child.**

. . .

Abelard: **Ellie?**

*

Heloise: **itcannotbe**

Abelard: **your uncle's kinsman**

Heloise: **say it wasnot**

Abelard: **my servant must have drugged me b4 sleep**

Heloise: **not possible**

Abelard: **a cord wound tightly around my scrotum**

Heloise: **wake me**

Abelard: **2 quick incisions**

Heloise: **mygod**

Abelard: **to prevent the wrong animal from breeding, they said**

Heloise: **THEY are the animals!**

Abelard: **i felt practically nothing.**

Heloise: **It is they who are not fit to be called human!**

Abelard: **the 2 who could be caught were blinded, and mutilated as I was**

Heloise: It is not enough. Sweet Jesus, it is not enough!

Abelard: the agony now is not for the mutilation of my body

Heloise: who tends you? you must not be alone.

Abelard: but rather the shame and humiliation

Heloise: The shame is not yours!

Abelard: All of Paris talks of it. Of us. How can I show my face in public, to be pointed at by every finger, derided by every tongue?

Heloise: I love you, Peter.

Abelard: My old, embittered teacher, Roscelin, has already written me. He starts by refusing to call me Peter, as it is a masculine name 'no longer appropriate'. And he warns of the other appendages I could yet lose: my 'tail of impunity' and my 'stinging tongue'.

Heloise: Listen to me. I love you. I have never loved you more.

Abelard: He spouted scripture. 'No man whose testicles have been crushed or whose organ has been severed shall become a member of the assembly of the Lord.'

Heloise: Stop this!

Abelard: Whereas Fulk writes to tell me to take comfort – notwithstanding 'the small' loss I have suffered – for I may now apparently walk 'safe and sinless' among virgins and no

husband will fear me. And the worst of it, of course, is he's right!

Heloise: u r not urself.

Abelard: I cannot bear the thought that another will have you.

Heloise: Then cease thinking it now.

Abelard: I want you to understand. There is no other course for us.

Heloise: What are you talking about?

Abelard: I have thought it all through.

Heloise: All what through?

Abelard: You must take the veil.

Heloise: ???

Abelard: Understand me.

. . .

Heloise: For disguise . . .

Abelard: It is for the best.

Heloise: En route to Brittany. Of course. We go to your brother's? I can be ready in a matter of hours. After all, does my uncle imagine I will return to his house?!

Abelard: **There will be no disguise. No escape to Brittany this time. You will give yourself to Christ.**

. . .

Abelard: **I too will take up orders.**

Heloise: **Stop this!**

Abelard: **You are surprised.**

Heloise: **Do you think I will be parted from you?!**

Abelard: **And do you think I will stay in society to be a monstrous spectacle to all I meet?!**

Heloise: **yougivemeaway**

Abelard: **Retreat is the only option.**

Heloise: **no**

Abelard: **You would choose the world rather than be true to me?**

Heloise: **u r halfmadwithmisery and now u madden me with it**

Abelard: **You deny me. When all is bad enough.**

Heloise: **i don't know what i do**

*

Confessions.com Clearing Your Conscience For You
Just Click on the Confessional Box

Should–Have–Known–Susan: I had my first baby four months ago. Nobody mentioned certain postnatal surprises at the time. Bladder control, for example. I was rushing through my local K–Mart when suddenly the floodgates opened in Home Electronics. I was horrified – had to make a dash for the main doors and leave the poor staff to assume a small child was responsible.

Absolution (Post your comments now.)
Coolcuke: Let it go. (No pun intended.)
Justjanice: Someone should have told you. That's plain poor after–care.
Cellogirl: I know we're not talking the same thing exactly but my waters broke during (get this) a performance of Handel's Water Music. No word of a lie. Just when I thought I couldn't be more embarrassed, the lead violinist slipped in it and fell.

*

Double–take Tim: I've been dating my girlfriend for three months now. I'm 35 and, as of now, sh**ing myself. Just found out: today's her birthday. Her 16th.

Absolution (Post your comments now.)
Hellsangel: Rock on, Tim.
Ratman: Lock up your daughters! Tim's in town.
Coolcuke: I can give you the number of a good lawyer, Tim. After that, you're on your own.
Foxysister: What was your first clue? When she started singing, 'I Am Sixteen Going on Seventeen'? Duh.

*

Abe: I cannot, like Tim, claim ignorance. There was in Paris a young woman named Heloise . . . I came to an arrangement with her uncle, with the help of some of his friends, whereby he should take me into his house, for whatever sum he liked to ask. As a pretext I said my household cares were hindering my studies. He was all eagerness for my money and confident that his niece would profit from my teaching. Her studies allowed us to withdraw in private, as love desired, and then with our books open before us, more words of love than of our reading passed between us. My hands strayed oftener to her bosom than to the pages.

In time, the girl found that she was pregnant, and immediately wrote me a letter full of rejoicing to ask what I thought she should do. When our baby son was born, we trusted him to my sister's care in Brittany and returned secretly to Paris, but word was out. We had been discovered. So I removed H to a convent of nuns so she might escape the fury of her uncle's temper. Yet, with the discovery of her whereabouts, he and his kinsmen and followers imagined that I had tricked them, and had found an easy way of ridding myself of Heloise by making her a nun. Wild with indignation they swore an oath against me, and one night as I slept they cut off the parts of my body whereby I had committed the wrong of which they complained.

Heloise agreed to take the veil in obedience to my wishes. There were many people, I remember, who in pity for her youth tried to dissuade her from submitting to the yoke of monastic rule as a penance too hard to bear, but all in vain. Admittedly, it was shame and confusion in my remorse and misery, rather than any devout wish for conversion, which brought me to take shelter in a monastery cloister.

Absolution (Post your comments now.)
Hellsangel: Ouch.
Chipofftheoldblock: French girl. Way to go.
Darklady: And you made her end her days in a convent
***because* . . . ?**

The Late EMails

To my shining light, my solstice,
You know, beloved, as everyone knows, how much I have lost in you,
how at one wretched stroke of fortune that supreme act of flagrant
treachery robbed me of my very self in robbing me of you; and how
my sorrow for my loss is nothing compared with what I feel for the
manner in which I lost you. Surely the greater the cause for grief the
greater the need for the help of consolation, and this no one can
bring but you; you are the sole cause of my sorrow, and you alone
can grant me the grace of consolation. You alone have the power
to make me sad, to bring me happiness or comfort; you alone have
so great a debt to repay me, particularly now when I have carried
out all your orders so implicitly that, when I was powerless to
oppose you in anything, I found strength at your command to destroy
myself.

I changed clothing along with my mind, in order to prove you the sole
possessor of my body and will alike. It was not any sense of vocation
which brought me to accept the austerities of the cloister, but your
bidding alone. If I deserve no gratitude from you, you may at least
judge for yourself how my labours are in vain. I can expect no reward
for this from God, for it is certain that I have done nothing as yet for
love of him. When you hurried towards God I followed you. Indeed, I
went first to take the veil. Your lack of trust in me over this one thing,
I confess, overwhelmed me with grief and shame. I would have had no
hesitation, God knows, in following you or going ahead at your bidding

to the flames of Hell. My heart was not in me but with you, and now, even more, if it is not with you, it is nowhere truly. Without you it cannot exist.

God knows I never sought anything in you except yourself. I beg you, think what you owe me, give ear to my pleas, and I will finish a long e-missive with a brief ending: farewell, my only love.
H.

*

To my sister in Christ,
If since our conversion from the world to God I have not yet written you any word of comfort or advice, it must not be attributed to indifference on my part but to your own good sense, in which I have always had such confidence that I did not think anything else was needed. If, in your humility, you feel that you have need of my instruction and writings in matters pertaining to God, write to me what you want, so that I may answer as God permits me.
Your loving brother

*

Peter,
Of all wretched women, I am the most wretched, and amongst the unhappy I am unhappiest. The higher I was exalted when you preferred me to all other women, the greater my suffering over my own fall and yours, when equally I was flung down; for the higher the ascent, the heavier the fall. If only your love had less confidence in me, so that you would be more concerned on my behalf!

I can find no penitence whereby to appease God, whom I always accuse of the greatest cruelty in regard to this outrage. By rebelling against his ordinance, I offend him more by my indignation than I placate him by making amends through penitence. How can it be called repentance for sins, if the mind still retains the will to sin and is on fire with its old desires? It is easy enough for anyone to confess his sins, to accuse himself, or even to mortify his body in outward show of penance, but it is very difficult to tear the heart away from hankering after its dearest pleasures.

In my case, the pleasures of lovers which we shared have been too sweet – they cannot displease me, and can scarcely shift from my memory. Wherever I turn, they are always there before my eyes, bringing with them awakened longings and fantasies which will not let me sleep. Even during the celebration of the Mass, when our prayers should be pure, lewd visions of those pleasures take such hold upon my unhappy soul that my thoughts are on their wantonness instead of prayer. I should be groaning over the sins I have committed, but I can only sigh for what I have lost. Everything we did and also the times and places where we did it are stamped on my heart along with your image, so that I live through them all again with you. Even in sleep I know no respite. Sometimes my thoughts are betrayed in a movement of my body, or they break out in an unguarded word.

Men call me chaste; they do not know the hypocrite I am. I can win praise in the eyes of men but deserve none before God, who searches our hearts and loins and sees in our own darkness. To me your praise is all the more dangerous because I welcome it. I beg you, be fearful for me always, instead of feeling confidence in me, so that I may always find help in your solicitude.

Yours, ever,
H.

*

Ellie,
Accept his will. You must understand that it has been most salutary for me – and will be for you too, if your transports of grief will see reason.

All that came upon us came upon us justly, as well as to our advantage and I will prove it to you now.

When you were living in hiding in the cloister, beyond your uncle's reach, you know what my uncontrollable desire did with you there, actually in a corner of the refectory, since we had nowhere else to go. I repeat, you know how shamelessly we behaved on that occasion in so hallowed a place, dedicated to the most holy Virgin. Even if our shameful behaviour at that time was all, this alone would deserve far heavier punishment. Need I recall our previous fornication and the wanton impurities, when I deceived your uncle about you so disgracefully, at a time when I was continuously living with him in his own house? Who would not judge me justly betrayed by the man whom I had first shamelessly betrayed? Do you think that the momentary pain of that wound is sufficient punishment for such crimes?

And so it was wholly just and merciful – although by means of the supreme treachery of your uncle – for me to be reduced in that part of my body which was the seat of my lust and sole reason for those desires.

You know too how when you were pregnant and I took you to Brittany you disguised yourself in the sacred habit of a nun, a pretence which was an irreverent mockery of the religion you now profess. Consider, then, how fittingly divine justice brought you against your will to the religion which you did not hesitate to mock. See how greatly the Lord was concerned for us, as if he were reserving us for some great ends, and was indignant or grieved because our knowledge of letters, the talents which he had entrusted to us, were not being used to glorify his name.

My love, which brought us both to sin, should be called lust, not love. Notwithstanding that, whatever is yours cannot, I think, fail to be mine, and mine, yours. Christ is yours because you have become his bride, and I praise God for it. All along, it was he who truly loved you, not I.

Your servant in Christ,
P.

*

You are cruel. You are cruel in order to teach me to accept a situation we cannot alter. I know you. Even now I know you. Your case is sound, yet it serves only to remind me how our words and logic have failed. So I whisper these last tender syllables.

I am with you until you fall asleep, even as you once said. I am inside your breast for ever.

Be not bereft.
H.

Dirty Weekend

Paris 2001

Easter weekend. We were lucky to get a room.

At reception, Monsieur can hardly bring himself to look up. He has already noted the grizzled and wind-blown mane of your hair. He observes the stains on your jacket and the regrettably wide lapels. His greeting is tepid, and my good French does not mollify. He passes us a key with few words, and we cross to the lift where you hit all the buttons at once, imitating, as the doors close, the sour twist of Monsieur's face. Indeed, so occupied are you by your performance that you fail to notice the doors have opened again.

At the desk, Monsieur is watching us with masterly sangfroid.

So I am not surprised that the room smells of cigarettes. Or that the paint is blistering. Or that there is an empty, still lubricated, condom packet under one corner of the bed. We peer around the bathroom door – the shower drain seems to double as a toilet – and we retreat again. I unzip my bags. Behind me, the wardrobe lists like a drunk. Whenever you pass it on the way to the window, its door flies open, as if a body is about to tumble out.

Never mind, we say. Never mind. We've made it. Paris. The trees in bud. The wind, gusty off the Seine, blowing off winter. You are as happy and insistent as a child. You give me ten minutes to unpack and mop up my eye infection while you calm yourself with a Hamlet on the street below. Then out.

On the other side of the street, across a large junction consti-pated with traffic, there's a brasserie too basic in its offerings to tempt anyone other than locals. 'Our brasserie,' you say, grinning, your dark Irish eyes alight. 'As of now, it's our brasserie. Everyone else can say au revoir toot de sweet.' You turn to me, screwing up your eyes up as if measuring the situation. 'Or not. Should we let the fuckers stay? Are we in a holiday mood?'

'We are.' I take your arm. 'I'd say we are.'

Inside, we relax in the dense and familial cloud of smoke. I sip my espresso. You light up. We toe each other under the table. To my left, a man with very small reading glasses and a gargantuan bottom orders coffee at the bar before spreading and smoothing his newspaper across one of the small black tables. He scans the room and spots something of interest by the window. It is not easy for him to manoeuvre his girth in the close confines of our little place, but we believe cosiness is what brings our customers back, time after time. He returns, panting slightly, with a second chair held at chest height. Then he seats himself or, more precisely, each buttock, one per chair.

I take a pen out of my bag. You are ready with a paper napkin. 'Forget *A Room of One's Own*,' I scribble. 'Think: *A Chair of One's Own*, the heretofore unpublished rallying cry of the anonymous buttock who would be ignored no longer.'

You take the pen and continue. 'The story of the buttock who yearned for café society, for romance, for a private income.' You glance, quickly, over your shoulder and shake your head, making a clicking noise with your mouth, as if to say, the news isn't good. 'Get a boil on that backside,' you write, recalling your own former plight, 'and we'll be looking at a *three*-chair outlay. For Christ's sake, does he think he's our only regular?'

The door opens and a four-foot-something-high woman with huge eyes and relentless eye-shadow walks in and joins the queue for cigarettes – 'Edith Piaf,' I write. You nod, nonchalant. The queue is restless, urgent, yellow-fingered. Edith is followed by a small man with an intelligent face and frizzy white wings of hair. We have run out of room on our napkin. 'I didn't know

Einstein frequented our brasserie,' I mumble through the side of my mouth.

You turn to look. 'Word gets round.' Then you smile, faux-smug, meaning, that's the kind of establishment you and I run.

That night, we run up rue de l'Odéon, looking for the ghost of Joyce. We lay hands on the green-painted brickwork of the shopfront that was once Sylvia B's. We talk dirty for Molly Bloom. We scoff at the hallowed Shakespeare & Co. and its grumpy owner who refused, on a sudden whim, to sell me the first-edition *Winter Pollen*. At last we walk back along the cold calm of the Seine, both of us wrapped in the bad fit of your jacket.

We sleep like apple seeds, bending towards one another. In the night, you knee me, sudden and hard in the stomach, and wake us both with the force of it. 'Sorry, darling. Sorry, sorry.' You were back in South Armagh, cornered. I stroke your head, rub your shoulders. In time, you turn me on to my other side and fold me against your chest.

In Montmartre, it's obscenely cold. I buy a scarf from a stall. A pashmina. Or a good fake, rather. Pale pink. You bundle me up in it and stow my hand in your coat pocket, wrapping my fingers in yours. On the steps of Sacré Coeur, we gorge on the views. It's Good Friday: pilgrim nuns wait on their knees as hundreds gather for the next Mass. We move on to the stairs but get no further than the wall of the faithful.

You, however, will not be deterred. You drop down a step and are suddenly at my back, pretending to take me from behind as you shunt me up the steps, one by one, against the press of the crowd. Inside, I find a space on one of the pews and fall into the trance of the Mass while you pace like something feral at the back of the nave. Later, we walk the seedy length of rue Pigalle, the neon sails of the Moulin Rouge spinning wearily in the night.

You cover my eyes, playing father while stocky men in bad suits tout for business outside clubs. 'Monsieur et Madame . . . ?' they inquire.

'Virgin!' you bark, nodding to me.

'Monsieur et Madame . . . ?'

'VIRGIN!' you shout. People stare, but you smile to yourself, your own happy Theatre of the Absurd.

As we approach the last suit, you consult me briefly on a point of vocabulary. 'Monsieur et Madame?' comes the call.

'VIERGE! ELLE EST VIERGE!' Then you turn to me, as if considering the prospect, and your eyebrows flicker darkly.

On Easter Saturday, it's the Gare-du-I-forget-which because you want to see the great surrealist heap of clocks outside the station. We stand before the twenty-foot tower and behold: dozens of clocks, black-rimmed, white-faced. Some, large and round, like those you'd find in an examination hall. Others, small and square – the no-nonsense bedside alarms of this world. It's as if clock after clock has been carelessly tossed on to the concrete plinth, from which one will at any moment fall, bringing down all of time with it.

It is five to ten. It is also twenty past eight, ten past seven, fourteen past three and twenty-one minutes to eleven; we take a strange comfort in the different lunatic time on each face. I dig for the camera and catch you in the viewfinder. You stand with your foot on the edge of the plinth, like a hunter with his foot on big game, as if you have overcome the merely chronological.

We lunch in the restaurant across the street where corpulent, Renoiresque couples enjoy weekend roasts and bonhomie. Is it that afternoon that we shop? Or rather, I shop and you recline, happy, easygoing, in a wicker chair, as I try on boas, scarves and chapeaux. A childish ritual but I am shameless.

Outside the shop, a small elderly man in a trench coat and black beret stops us. He takes my hand in his. He tells us we look so well together, so happy, he wanted to stop and say; he squeezes my hand and tells me he can't think when he saw so radiant a smile.

'Piss off,' you say as he moves out of earshot, but your grin is irrepressible. Your chest swells. You cock your head slightly, awaiting tacit acknowledgement that you are indeed responsible for the purported radiance of my smile. But you have your principles. You won't have us turned into an old man's grainy monochrome. You won't have us consigned to a perfect moment, already gone.

We count bashed cars – every fourth, we estimate. Sideswiped. One after the other. Why can't the French drive? For that matter, you inquire, why can't they walk? It's a fair question. People keep knocking into you. On the Metro. At street corners. At the weekend market on Ile St Louis. As we eat glazed raspberry tarts on the Champs Élysées. On top of the Arc de Triomphe in face-flattening winds. 'And do they say, pardonnez-moi?' you ask. 'Noooo. Do they say, excuse me please for being a rude mother-fucker? No, I say. Non!' You laugh but your indigestion is sharp again. We find a pharmacy, the second time since we have arrived.

It's when the pain is easing that we spot Picasso, circa 1965, emerging from the Metro on the Champs-Élysées. 'Regardes!' you say.

I dab at my leaking eyes and squint into the wind. 'Mais oui,' I breathe. 'Monsieur Picasso lui-même.'

We are inspired by this chance encounter with celebrity and take it as a sign. We rush down the stairs to the Metro and jump, on faith, on to a train. We arrive at Place de la Concorde – several changes and over two hours later. We don't have a sense of direction between us.

Under a marquis adjunct at the Jeu de Paume, the queue for tickets is long but restrained. This is Paris. Everyone shuffles forward with an elegant ennui. You self-medicate with a cigar and try not to fidget. I reach for my drops and tip my head back. 'There, there,' you say, patting my back as my eyes stream. 'Don't cry.' People turn in the queue. You take my face between your hands. You wipe away my artificial tears. You look me in the eye, imploringly. 'I *told* you, we can't. *Not* in public.'

We walk at last into the ponderous hush of the temple. Exhibition-goers, with half-moon glasses and po-faces, scrutinize the dirty art of the man. 'Picasso: érotique.' We laugh. From the belly.

Because it seems counter the spirit of the work *not* to go tee-hee; *not* to point. Not to think, *yes*. Doesn't the work itself extol irreverence? Doesn't it say stop fretting? Here, at least, in your own skin, stop fretting. Here, if nowhere else. And I remind you of your bravura at the old Tate – chasing me up the stone steps, barking and biting my bottom while a group of Japanese young people looked on, startled. You laugh, shy at the memory of your own antics but rather pleased I have not forgotten.

I love the drawing of the standing woman with the blue mackerel suspended between her legs, its long, fishy tongue tickling the dark opening of her. You are amused by the drawings of Gauguin and Degas at the brothel and peep-show: the artist as puny, smutty voyeur. Above all, we love the minotaurs. Especially '*Minotaure caressant du mufle la main d'une femme endormie.*' I can see him still: the terrific bulk of his head; the pubic wooliness of the fur around his horns; the hump of muscle at his back (the same as yours in bed next to me); the wild dashes of hair at the base of his back and under his arm; the horned awkwardness of his feet; his tender crouch over the sleeping woman; his inability not to touch her sleeping face.

You tell me you've had trouble with horn recently.

'The horn?' I say, casually.

'No. *Horn.*'

I look at my nails. 'Really . . . ?' I will not yet concede interest.

Here, here on our holiday, everything fabulous must also be made true.

You fold your arms across your chest. 'Horn can be the unfortunate by-product of an untreated fungal infection.'

My face tells you you'll need to do better than that.

So you begin again. 'The truth is, fungus is a funny thing. No, not funny. Stealthy. It creeps up on you – all too literally. What then? I'll tell you what then. Infection breaks out. No problem, you think. The foot grows new skin to cover the infected area. Only it's still there. Below. While you might think you smell it, you don't see it – and *that's* your undoing. You persuade yourself it's gone. Over. Adios, amigo. But what happens? The bastard fungi break through again. Another layer grows for cover. So you get one layer after another after another, because you always think something will go away in the end, don't you, if you wait it out, if you stare evil down. But, all the time, unknown to anyone, those layers are compacting, little by little, because you're walking on them all the time – am I right? – pressing them into something less than human, something that no pumice stone will stand up to. God knows I tried, God knows I did, and Jesus himself wept with it and all the angels and all the self-flagellating, hair-shirted, strap-me-to-a-wheel-and-pierce-me saints. But it's too late. Too late. Which is a hard-won wisdom. Because already, already, there at the bottom of your Marks & Spencer's size-seven-to-ten, eighty-denier sock, you've got a god-damned, skip-along-with-Pan hoof in the making.'

I want to clap.

You confess it took several trips to the foot clinic to render you human again. I make the sign of the cross in the air before you, and the horn-footed demon in you is released. Absolved. Free, like us, to grab an overpriced cup of museum coffee and a tough croissant.

Later, back in our shabby room, we curl close for a nap but

can't sleep. Picasso, the dirty bugger, has left us brimming with too much life. We're fertile. Rampant. Tender. We negotiate your sensitive stomach, and sleep at last, wrapped in each other's scent.

The next day – Versailles. Rain and monumental stone. We succumb to the tour. I wish we hadn't. You open a door marked ENTRÉE INTERDITE and are given a sharply whispered warning by the guide. You blush in spite of yourself.

Outside, you pose for photographs, serious, aristocratic. You cock your chin like an Empire Man in front of fountains, statuary and boxed hedges. You speak mock French behind a group of Latvian tourists. You are overcome by sudden courtliness and get down on one knee in the middle of a pebbled path. 'I want you to know,' you say.

'Know what?' I say, checking the schedule for trains back.

'That I will go down on my knees for you.' You grin briefly, but behind the performance is something else. You don't jump again to your feet. You stay there, shifting on your knee, staring up at me from the middle of the path. 'I want you to know.'

I smile at my middle-aged lover. 'Beautiful man,' I mouth.

The sun is going down. The wind is sharpening. We retrace our steps over the cobbles and through the gate. 'Will I ever be here again?' he says.

'I don't know,' I say, determinedly offhand. 'Will you?' There is no audience. I will not allow melodrama.

Brighton 2003

The Old Ship. Room 222. We open the door to the novelty of twin beds and NO SMOKING. I manage to heave up the begrudging sash, shift the breakfast table, and position the chair by the window so you can exhale smokily into the evening beyond.

It is cool for August. The sea is already dark, choppy. The helter-skelter at the end of the pier stands bright, a crazy, candy-striped monument to chaos. The lights of the prom are faint, tremulous, in the twilight. In the other direction, the West Pier is beautiful, ramshackle, degenerate. You can't stop looking.

Before the final op, the one that would sever the nerve from your liver and deaden, at long last, some of the pain, you were warned there were risks. There was a chance they might snip the wrong nerve. On top of everything else, you could end up unable even to walk. You could be in a wheelchair for the rest of your days.

Which were few.

But that wasn't it. 'Impotent,' you said. 'It could make me impotent.'

We'd last made love in January, in the euphoria of your supposed all-clear. Months ago now – for sex no longer seemed relevant. Yet you weren't worrying about the actual mechanics of desire. 'I don't want to lose it,' you said, your eyes filling. 'My libido.'

You didn't want to stop wanting.

Outside the Old Ship, night rolls in with the tide, and the seafront throbs with basslines that spill from open-top cars. From the window I watch a spiky huddle of lads on the bike path across the street. They're whistling and calling across traffic to three girls in dark tans and micro skirts. Eggs-on-legs, we used to call them fondly. Tonight they're on their way to the Escape or the Beach or the Honeyclub. In the dark of our room, you let your clothes fall from you and disappear below a thin blanket.

I close the window and draw the drapes. For a time, I watch TV with the sound off. When I ease myself into the narrowness of your bed, I am afraid I will bruise you. The hump of muscle at your back is gone. Your big chest is little more than the hull of your ribs. In the dark, you turn on to your side, hiding yourself.

I rub your shoulders and back and shins, as if you are a child who can't get off to sleep. 'Shall I go now?' I whisper. 'Let you sleep?'

'No . . .' I can hardly hear you.

So I press my breasts and stomach to your back, my thighs to the back of your thighs, and we lie close and still. Because I am damned if you will die feeling already dead.

It is late the next morning when I haul back the dark weight of the drapes. Even in the blast of sudden light, you do not wake. It will be after one before I can get you to sit up in bed. 'Do you want to go back?' I say. 'I can get the car.'

'No,' you insist, groggily. 'Brighton.' Each word is a triumph of concentration. 'Brighton. Our . . . dirty . . . weekend.'

I run the bath. You hang on to my neck as I lower you in. I wash your back. You tip your head, and I rub Old Ship shampoo into your ever wild head of hair; hair that not even the chemo could touch. I soap up your chest and stomach, and you yield to the massage, enjoying for these few minutes the pleasures of the flesh.

It takes me over an hour to dress you, and though I don't understand it as I labour over you, your legs have already started to stiffen and swell with death. Your shoes and socks no longer fit. You mumble instructions. 'Push. Push.' And, even as I do, you fall back on to the bed into sleep, unconsciousness pulling at you like a riptide.

By three, we make it out of the room and down to the ground floor – our destination, the Old Ship brasserie. '*Our* brasserie,' you pronounce as you collapse into a leather armchair, groping for the Hamlets in your shirt pocket.

You slurp cold, sugary tea. The contents of your cup spill into your saucer and over your shirt. I watch the cigar in your hand, collecting it quickly each time it falls to the floor.

Through the window beside us, all of life – bronzed workmen, face-painted children, pregnant mums, old men in motorized chairs, boys on the make, girls in bikini tops, small bridesmaids in lilac dresses, a couple in matching wetsuits, another couple, raw-faced with anger, bemused tourists and a man bearing a wet dog in his arms – through the window, all of life passes.

The afternoon I drive you home – the afternoon before the morning you will yield at last to the coma – you walk me, gripping the handrail, to the bottom of your long flight of stairs and hold fast to my hand as you see me on my way. Upstairs your daughter waits with your cup of tea and horde of pain-killers.

'You and me,' you slur.

'You and me,' I say, pressing your hand, kissing your neck.

'You've got that long drive,' you say.

I struggle with the latch on the Yale lock and pull the door open. 'I'll pop a CD in.' I hover at the threshold, not moving. It is impossible to pull away. Yet to stay, to not return to my flat as usual, to sleep in the place I soon will – on your attic floor near your sickbed – would be to tell you that you are about to die. And you, putting too much faith in my instinct, would believe me and begin to die. I can't risk it.

'We'll talk tonight?' You sway like a happy drunk.

'Same time,' I say.

'Listen,' you say.

'I'm listening,' I say.

'You're the only woman' – you have to pause to breathe – 'you're the only woman I'm going to god-damn *die* wanting,' and you smile.

Because you've managed it. You still *want*: me, me wanting you, a good smoke, a new book, long views, chance encounters, life – reckless and beloved – life on the hoof.

You kiss me.

'Horn,' you mumble.

'You and those feet of yours . . .'

'*No,*' you say, feigning exasperation. 'Horn.' Your eyelids flutter. I can smell the residue of the heroin as it exits your pores. '*The* horn.'

These days, you're searching for a title – any title you haven't read yet – among the stacks of your books in someone's garage, as if you're in bad need of distraction. Or I'm meeting you at Arrivals. It was a long journey back. You're stumbling through the double doors, rumpled in the linen suit I chose for your laying-out. You're gamely clutching your stitched-up groin, so happy to see me when you thought you were a goner. We hug, holding on, and something eases at last within both of us. Or you have a new mobile phone. You're waving it at me. 'See,' you're telling me. 'See. I can get you on this thing now.'

Sometimes too, in my mind's eye, I see us, the ghosts of us, still there, en route to Monsieur's hotel. They're peeking in windows along the way. They're turning a map right side up and upside down. Her eyes are streaming in the wind, and the map won't stay still. They cross the boulevard, zigzagging through traffic. 'C'mon!' he's shouting. He's got her by the hand. The street can't be far. They take the next corner, walking straight into the stiff gust that's blowing off the Seine. They're laughing as the breath is knocked out of them.

The Knowledge of Penises

That night, she felt all hole. Not legs and breasts and shoulders but, suddenly, all hole.

He felt her hands leaving him, her body shifting unexpectedly below his. He smelled the spiciness of her sweat as she reached into the big night of their bed; heard the familiar knock of her wedding ring against the pine headboard. Then: the pale flash of her inner arms in the darkness, and, quietly, so he had to strain to hear, 'Hold me down.'

She wanted to feel him tap her, the source within her. She wanted him to find the deep wishing well of her. But theirs was a different vocabulary – soft-lipped, deep-hearted, tender as palms, clean as his wide, white brow – and her words stained the air between them like sour breath.

In the small rented cottage, on her own, Nina finds herself thinking about the knowledge of penises.

In the back of her mind, she sketches them as primitive life forms: single-celled creatures who live, blind and unpigmented, in the pools of caves, sluggishly longing for transformation. She invests these penises with a slow, hesitant inner life and a flaccid intelligence, but with it an acute sensitivity to, an almost penitential longing for, change. For motion. And this moves her, deeply.

At other times, Nina's penises are tall and totem-like, rising above her like the dark, three-foot, slope-headed shadows the candelabra in her sitting room casts on to the whitewashed walls. Occasionally, she looks up from her book and thinks on the puzzle of them: how they seem to threaten and protect at the same time.

These are the penises, Nina tells herself, that, behind their single blind eyes, know the secret of change: they are tall and rigid with need. They're monuments to it.

Nina knows no one else thinks about the knowledge of penises. Except Tom. Tom is the son of her friend Marion. He is three years old. Twice a week, Nina and Marion spoon their worries into coffee cups and sip on them slowly.

Nina says, 'Tell him you get the mattress and he can have the bed frame.'

'Are you kidding? I can't get my scan pictures of Tom, let alone our mattress.' She looks up, her eyes straining against the tears. 'You're lucky, the way you and Mark can still talk.'

Nina doesn't feel lucky. These days, she feels unreal. Insubstantial.

Tom shouts from upstairs where he is building Lego towers. 'I'm going for a wee, Mummy!'

'Okay, Tom, but mind the toilet seat, all right?' Marion tilts her head and, with one ear, listens for trouble. 'It fell the other day and almost came down on his willie. He sort of rests it on the rim when he goes, and the seat's heavy, mahogany or something, and I said, "You be careful, Tom, or you'll lose it, you will." So he takes the matter very seriously now.' She dips a biscuit into her cup and looks at it pensively. 'You know, I miss the dining-room table even more than the bed. Six matching chairs. It was ever such a nice set. Pete got it at an auction. Distressed wood.' She turns to Nina, suddenly grinning like a schoolgirl. 'Least, that was his story. I should ring him and say, "Oy, Pete, give over. *How the fuck* did you manage to distress even fucking wood?"'

'All done, Mummy!'

Marion springs guiltily to her feet and shouts up the stairs. 'Good boy, Tom! Wash your hands now.' She gives Nina a wicked glance. 'Castration averted. The future of the race is safe.'

Nina feels invisible next to Marion and her brutish ex and

her single-motherhoodom and her girlish vulnerability. She and Mark are both such nice people, no one wants to know. And she doesn't really want anyone to know: that the hole within her is getting bigger and bigger.

'Hi, Tom,' she says. Tom has come down the stairs with a box of Lego and no underpants on. Marion laughs. 'Forget something?'

'No,' he says defiantly.

She makes a face of mock surprise at Nina. 'That's me told.'

He spills a torrent of Lego on to the carpet between Nina's feet and prances before her like a kid goat on hind legs.

'Another cup?' says Marion.

'If you're having one.'

Tom falls on to the floor by her feet. He pulls off her mules and wedges the smallest-sized bricks between her toes.

'Thomas, would you like a juice?'

'Don't *look* at me,' says Tom. It's the rule when he wants to play with Nina's feet, or hold her arm behind her back and probe its underside like a doctor, or remove mysterious instruments from her bag: an eyelash curler, a pair of tweezers, a nail file.

'Still this little game, eh, you?' smiles Nina. She makes light of it for Tom.

Marion shakes her head, bemused. 'Only with you.' She folds her arms across her chest. 'Juice or milk, Tom?'

'Milk.'

Nina knows already that Tom's game is only for her. She knows he likes touching her, bending her. She knows he knows he shouldn't and she wonders if she should put an end to it somehow, but she feels like his doll. A strange sort of yielding comes over her.

She looks down, studying him. He is poking the bare sole of her foot with a red Lego tower. He knows it hurts. He knows she won't stop him.

'Don't *look* at me!'

'All right, Tom,' and Nina looks away as Marion enters the room with two steaming mugs in one hand and Tom's milk in the other.

'Little fascist,' Marion declares under her breath, but she's smiling. 'I love the way children touch you. I love his little buttocks climbing in next to me in the mornings. Sometimes, he'll just lie there and play with my face and hair, won't you, Tom-Tom?'

Nina thinks about the human brain, about what they said on that programme the other week – how the largest areas of its labyrinthine surface are given over to the needs of just the face, the hands and the genitals. She wonders if that is how children first perceive the human form: a full moon of a face with wide, cartoon hands and mighty genitals where the heart, lungs and stomach should be.

He is behind her now, on the sofa, crouching at her back. She can feel him, tight as a spring. 'Tom,' says Marion, 'Nina has coffee. It's very hot. If you bump her, it will spill. Why don't you play on the floor?'

'I'll be very still,' he says.

Marion looks sceptical but is distracted by the phone. She picks it up, turns away. Nina watches her in profile. Sees her face going taut, white. Hears her voice disappear in her throat. 'I can't, Pete. You *know* why.'

Nina signals to her. *Do you want me to go?*

Marion frowns and shakes her head. 'I said I'm not. Don't shout. No, I'm telling you, there's no one here. Just Nina. We're having coffee . . . Yes. Here. Where else? He's playing with Nina.'

Behind her, Tom has Nina's free arm in his hands. He twists her wrist and pins it to the small of her back. When she lets it slip, he presses it roughly back into place and she does not try to move it again. He understands now that she understands. Nina sips her coffee.

'I'm just trying to be practical, Pete. If I did, I didn't mean to . . . I know you're his father . . .'

But now Tom's small hand is burrowing below her, pushing pieces of Lego between the sofa cushion and her buttocks. Through the cotton of her skirt, she can feel the thrusting of his small fisted hand. And still, one hand is pressed to her back while the other negotiates her coffee, and Tom, at her back, works the pieces of Lego beneath her: hard corners and lengths of plastic.

Marion is rubbing her forehead with the heel of her hand. 'I'm not lying . . .'

Nina looks down and suddenly finds Tom's small hands at either side of her, reaching for her thighs. He grabs a bunch of her skirt in either hand and begins to pull. Hard. For a moment, she is startled by the urgency of it; by the force of his childish sexuality, as yet unsublimated by rockets, fire ladders and the knots of school ties. Tom is all need, and his small hands are pummelling the tops of her thighs, forcing her skirt up.

Marion puts down the phone, and Nina wills herself off the sofa. 'Are you all right?' she hears herself say.

'I hung up on him. He wouldn't stop. I just put the phone down.' She remembers Tom. Turns round to him. Stares, glassy-eyed, as if nothing makes sense any more. He is standing on the sofa, a red Lego tower forced over the top of his small erect penis.

'Tom, take that off right now.'

'Don't look at me. No one can *look* at me!'

'I've had enough of this today. Take that off right now! If you can't play nicely, you can play upstairs by yourself.' She sighs and begins scooping up the Lego. 'Sorry, Nina. I'd laugh if –'

'I know. I should go.' Nina hadn't realized small boys could have erections. She imagined their testicles had to drop first.

'I *am* tired.'

'You must be.'

'Say goodbye to Nina, Tom.'

But Tom says nothing. His face is red, primitive. The small finger of his penis points at her as she picks up her bag and disappears behind her sunglasses, traitorous.

Once a week, Nina and Mark meet for lunch or dinner. It's a chance to remember one another for one another. A mutual kindness. These days, they both feel they are disappearing from the world.

They hug, closely. They order wine, bread baked in a wood fire, goat's cheese tartlets, a rocket salad with two forks, grilled salmon for him and primavera for her. The waitress smiles as she reverses glasses and lays bright silver. She admires the deep red of Nina's silk blouse. 'Vermilion,' she observes. 'You don't often see it,' and, for a moment, she is intent on Nina, as if she is a Sign. Of a wound to come, or a passion soon to enter her life.

The waitress pours the Pinot Grigio and hears the man tell his companion that he has a new poem he'd like her to look at. She notices he bites his nails to the quick, which endears him to her as she eavesdrops. She might be sceptical about the poetry if it weren't for those bitten nails, and his hands. He has generous hands. The waitress imagines Mark and Nina in an Umbrian villa in April; in a croft in the Western Isles at Christmas; at an intimate London club at New Year. Nina and Mark are the bright, transparent vessels of the dreams of others, still.

After talk of his family and the absence of each other's books and her pension worries and the ache they each wake with, Mark says, 'I need to tell you something.'

She looks up; takes the last sip of wine from her glass. She can't bear the thought of him on the end of a hook. 'Are you sleeping with her?'

He nods, looking at the remnant of salad on his plate.

'It's . . . good, isn't it? You wouldn't need to tell me otherwise.'

'It's early days.'

She thinks of his penis, a magician's bouquet for this new woman. 'We'll still see each other sometimes?' she asks.

He nods and remembers his voice: 'Yes. *Of course.*' Then he helps her into her jacket, lifting her hair where it is trapped at the collar.

Even now it is natural to her – like a musical ear or a green thumb or healing hands is natural to others. Nina brings people to life. She can show people the self they dream of being. She can return them to the person they once were. It has something to do with the quality of her attention. That which is inert, inanimate or impotent moves for her, like the loop of a snake in a basket.

Strangers fall in love with her easily for this reason. Both sexes. The occasional gay man. Her students. Distant colleagues she passes in the common room at work. Dusty men in paper shops. Old people longing in the twilight at bus stops. Breathless children. The man who came to fix her computer and lingered over its keys, as if her hands were still there. Telesalesmen who digress, listening for the lilt of her voice.

But there is something more to her gift, something primitive that requires an idol or a talisman – like when a door used to need a horseshoe before it was opened to receive the first guest. A horseshoe, not because it was a horseshoe, but a horseshoe because, upside down, it was black and of fire, and bad luck too but, with all those things, those risks, it was also finally the shape of a woman inside. Even if long forgotten. Even if people nowadays prefer door knockers to horseshoes. Nina understands this, the force of the primitive. And wordlessly, she also understands that her gift needs the power of that single blind eye longing within her.

So she almost blames herself. Did part of her conjure the man on the side of the road that afternoon?

The WPC at her door is young, broad-hipped, reassuringly

sturdy. On the phone earlier, they had asked her if she would prefer a WPC, and she had said, 'No, I really don't mind,' but felt she'd disappointed them in some way. That really she should have preferred a woman. So she'd made sure the kettle was boiled and, as she heard the officer come up the path, she was poised to ask her if she'd like a cup of tea, because that was what they did on TV, and when she did, she was relieved by the officer's enthusiasm.

'And how do you feel now?' WPC French studies Nina kindly between sugary sips.

'Okay,' says Nina. 'I mean, I am now. Not that anything actually happened.'

'All the same, it must have been very –'

'Yes,' says Nina, wondering if she still looks like she has been crying; remembering how the tears had started to well within her as she'd climbed into the Land Rover she'd flagged down; how the woman driver's wide blue eyes had told Nina that she was not as composed, not as matter-of-fact, in her account as she'd hoped. 'Sorry,' Nina had said to her through the partially rolled-down window, 'would you mind just taking me around the next bend? Sorry. It's just that that man back there . . .'

The woman's husband was in the back seat with a white bundle of a new baby on the seat next to him. Through the rear window, he looked warily at the unexpected vision of Nina in her sunglasses, shorts and tank top – there was never anyone on this road, only farm vehicles.

She tried again. 'I think he was waiting there for me.' She didn't know how else to say it, to this solid Sunday couple and their baby, new as hope, in the back seat: 'He had an erection. In his hands.' She couldn't let them drive away.

'Before I forget,' says WPC French, 'you'll be hearing from Victim Support. It's part of procedure now. Just so you know.'

Nina nods. Am I a victim now? she wonders.

WPC French reaches for forms and a pen, and Nina rises from

her seat to hit the light switch. The electric candelabra throws its three-foot penis shadows on to the walls around them. Then she is describing the black hatchback parked at the side of the green and winding lane, where she'd first seen it – seen him, he was only young – and how she'd felt a bad hum inside her, like a note struck on a cracked tuning fork.

'It's a three-mile loop, the walk I take,' she explains. (The walk she takes to help fill up her evenings and weekends; to remember her body; to teach her bewildered brain that she is indeed alone.) 'After he'd spotted me, he drove around the opposite way, I suppose to take me by surprise on the road up ahead.'

'How many minutes up ahead?'

'On foot? Ten, I'd say.'

'And you recognized the car as you approached it the second time?'

'Yes. It was parked again, facing me, somewhere beyond the last house in the village. At the crest in the road.'

'So this is farmland now?'

'Yes.' And she remembers. The flayed fields. The harvest, gone. Only seagulls scrabbling in the turned earth for sudden worms.

'And as you approached?'

She felt something was wrong, or about to go wrong; she carried on though because, 'You think it's just your imagination, don't you?' A car passed, an old banger, with a girl at the wheel and a young man next to her. They were laughing. She was pretty, with lots of dark hair. They looked like lovers on a Sunday drive as they passed both her and the black hatchback before disappearing around the bend.

She read the front plate of his car easily. And it seemed as if she had plenty of time to come up with a picture to match the three letters, to hear a certain music in the rhythm of the three numbers. It all seemed to be unfolding slowly and deliberately, as if she were walking into a scene she was inventing with every step.

She could see the top of his head now, behind the open hatchback. He was out of the car. Yet as she neared the car, not ten feet from him, she told herself not to be silly. He was only getting something out of the boot. A spare tyre. Or a bottle of motor oil. She worried fleetingly about the rise and fall of her breasts in her tank top. She never met anyone out here; had thought only about the Indian-summer heat that baked the road at midday.

She glanced his way, ready to nod, when he turned towards her. Seagulls in the field ahead swept chaotically into flight. She didn't understand – thought, what *is* that in his hands?

'I'm sorry to have to ask you this, but they're all different, you know. Could you describe it? Any marks? Tattoos? Piercings? Was it big or small?'

'Big. It looked very big.' Nina feels like a child. 'It was fat. Also.' She tries to find appropriate words. 'Thick. In circumference.'

'Could you estimate its length in inches?'

Nina imagines an identity parade of erections. Big ones. Small ones. Some purple-headed. Some pinky white. Circumcised. Column-like. Club-like. 'I'm really not very good on measurements.'

'So he turned to you, was watching you, and . . . ?'

'He started rubbing himself –'

'Can you be more specific?'

'He started rubbing his penis with one hand while holding it at the base with the other.' Yes. Two hands around it, and him stoop-backed, as if it were a weighty offering.

'And that's when he started shouting?'

'Yes.'

'Shouting or grunting?'

'Moaning.' Moans so loud, they filled up the emptiness of the fields as she walked away from him. They followed her up the road, insisting at her back; reminding her that there was no one there but the two of them.

'A real exhibitionist.'

'I guess so.' But there was more to it. She has heard people through hotel room walls; once, from the echoing darkness of a waiting room on a train platform; and in films, of course, where men rarely cry out.

Nina knows and doesn't want to know. She knows that he was making himself a monument to need; that his penis was tall and strong with it. That he became larger than life on that crest of road, crying out, mouthing himself into being between the laid-bare fields of September.

'If I'd stumbled upon him, it would have been almost laughable.' She imagines this is what a single woman of the world would say in these circumstances. She feels oddly two-dimensional. 'What bothered me was the way he seemed to be lying in wait for me – not that he was waiting for *me*. Obviously it could have been any woman.'

She is lying. A part of her fears that, on seeing her, he knew it had to be her; that that single blind eye sensed her passing. Knew like Marion's Tom knew. Like Mark never did. About the all-hole of her. The source. The deep wishing well within her.

WPC French is telling her they might contact her again; that they might have further questions; that she might be asked to testify in court. She asks her to read the statement she has prepared. She indicates where Nina is to sign at the bottom of each page and thanks her for the tea.

When WPC French is gone, she switches off the overhead light and sits in the memberless dark.

Nina still walks that wide, wide loop out of the village and through the open farmland. Sometimes she hears again the riot of his need filling the fields around her, but she walks on.

It's September. An Indian summer. Still hot, even come evening. Today she is catching the last of the light. A walk after work. Before supper. Then, as usual, radio, book, bath and bed.

She knows every bend, every stray sheep, every broken bit of fence. She notices the box and tin cup are still tied to the rusty table at the end of the farm path. In the summer, there are border plants here and home-grown tomatoes with a sign to put money please in the cup. But the box is empty now. She picks up the tin cup and dips a finger in the rainwater as if it might once have been water from a holy well and this, a place for offerings.

She has nothing.

It's true, she and Mark still meet for lunch or dinner, and love one another as well as their new lives allow. She and Marion drink coffee, though less often now. Tom grows – taller every time she sees him. Occasionally, she feels the surprise of his little hand up her dress; he presses it to her bottom, quickly, as if her buttock is a hot stove. Marion has a new man. He laughs easily. He touches her as if he has always been touching her; as if he always will be. Marion looks beautiful.

Nina carries on, past the stables where a horse is panicking on the other side of the hedge; past the derelict bathtub at the corner of the field that the sheep use as a trough. She notices the sun falling from the sky.

She comes to the narrowest point on the road, where the young trees meet overhead to make a low, leafy bower. She passes under, moving into sudden darkness. It will be a minute yet before she can see through to the other side. She thinks, it is like when you know you are about to wake up but haven't quite.

Then, through this lucid dream of green darkness, she sees them. Splashes of colour. Red, white, purple, blue, deep pink. She blinks as she emerges from the tunnel. Balloons. Dozens of them. Tied to a large gate, the gateposts, the nearby trees – and tied with wit. Pairs of big-nippled pink breasts bounce on the breeze. A long, purple, single-eyed penis nods to her from an overhanging branch, erect on a throne of twin testicles. She smiles.

From somewhere behind the adjacent house she hears a far-away salvo of corks popping and sudden raucous laughter.

There is no one in sight. She reaches high. One balloon, she tells herself, will not be missed.

By the time she arrives home, it is already dark. The evening star trembles above the cottage as she pulls the heavy door to – she likes its bad fit. And the heavy, ancient key. And the wrought-iron ring of a knocker to which she has just tied the single balloon.

Why?

Why not? she asks herself.

Nor will she give it a second thought after she turns the key for the night. She will heat up some soup in a pan, make a fire in the vast grate, turn on Radio 4 and, later, run a bath, heedless of the long balloon nudging the night beyond, dowsing blindly for any breath of wind – ignorant of everything but motion.

Pilot

As we came together, as you moved above me, I remembered only then, in the hot, still spaces between our breaths.

an undertow   I was   I was in the undertow   climbing for air
when something nosed me   up

into the air   into the brightness

back to shore
my limbs driftwood in the surf   my lungs sponge
white sand spilled from my mouth

but life   life again
as it came deep into me   my arms moving to encircle it   to hold
it fast

an oiled muscle of a back   an   an exhortation
of such love

that I was suddenly awake and wet salt water still
on my lips.

'You were crying,' you said as I woke, your face looming over mine.

I surfaced slowly, blinking.

'What's up?' You smoothed my hair on the pillow.

'Nothing.'

'Sure?'

'Sure I'm sure.'

You kissed my wet lashes. 'Twenty minutes till the alarm,' you said with a grin and opened the bedside drawer.

I wiped my face in my hands and rolled towards you as you

struggled with the box. 'Give it here,' I said. I slid a nail under the tight folds of cellophane. You stroked my belly. Then you were over me, and it was then: I remembered . . . climbing for air, something nosing me into the brightness, and life, life again as my arms moved to encircle it.

Later, I heard the flush, and behind closed eyes, I saw the condom carried through pipes the size of a whale's arteries into the amniotic sea. From below the ebb and flow of the quilt, I called to you, 'Come here. Come back to bed. Your father can open up today.' But my stomach was tight with a sense of betrayal I couldn't define, and already you were rubbing your face and armpits with a towel, and shaking your foreskin dry.

'How do you know?'
  'I know.'
  'I said, how, Helen?'
  'The line turned blue.'
  'Do it again.'
  'I've already done it again.'
  'But we used a –'
  'My nail must have caught it.'
  'You've been late before.'
  'But the line turned –'
  'Then you're doing it wrong.'
  'You're angry.'
  'Let me see the stick.'
  'I threw it out.'
  'When?'
  'Yesterday, at work.'
  'You're not pregnant.'
  'You *are* angry.'
  'Where are my keys?'
Then you were gone, I didn't know where, till finally your father brought you home long after dark, stinking of woodsmoke

and whisky. He shrugged at me and looked at the kitchen lino. 'Congratulations,' he whispered, taking my hand in his calloused palm. 'That's fine news.'

'Is it?' I asked, nodding to the sofa where you'd collapsed.

'He'll come round. You wait.'

For years, he had bullied you when you'd explained that there was no hurry for a family. I'd smile weakly as you made your point – my put-upon smile you called it – and I'd say nothing when your father asked what on earth was wrong with you.

You'd known what I wouldn't admit: with a baby, you'd find yourself even more alone than you already were.

When I miscarried at eight weeks – dark clots of blood at the bottom of the toilet, one the size of a pudding bowl – my doctor reassured me. She said I was fine, that there was no infection, that we'd be able to try again. She said that an early miscarriage was nature's way of ensuring the health of both mother and infant. 'But I've been so well,' I told her. 'I've been exercising and –'

'It isn't your fault,' she said.

'I lost the baby.'

'The foetus might have implanted at an unsuitable site. Or the chromosomes may have been problematic.'

'Problematic how?'

'Impossible to say. But miscarriages are sometimes caused by abnormal chromosomes so that a foetus, which would not have developed normally, is simply discarded.'

I wanted to say it wasn't simple, nothing was simple, but I could only stare at the unreadable hieroglyphs of her eye chart on the back wall.

'Do you have any questions?'

'Yes.' I looked up, surprised by the directness of my own voice. But no words came, and I wondered myself what I had meant.

You'd told me to phone you after the appointment. You

wanted to know what the doctor said. But I didn't. What was the hurry? You'd believed in the baby too late.

Instead I parked the Bookmobile on the dead-end road beyond the video store. I locked the door from the inside and lifted out the 1976 biology textbook from under my desk. I turned to page 223 and fingered the black-and-white picture of an X-ray: a life-sized human foetal skeleton, curled like an ammonite. I read again the tiny print below picture 4a.

At eight weeks, it is possible to detect a foetal heartbeat. However, recognizable signs of human life, such as fingers, toes, external genitalia and facial features will not be evident until the end of the first trimester. The student will note that, at this stage, it is indeed difficult to distinguish between the foetus of a human and that of a fish. See 4b. Both are characterized by the curved spinal column, the rudimentary tail, and the same fine deposit of cranial bone, which, in the human foetus, will form part of the internal ear, and in the fish foetus, the gill apparatus.

Whales are not fish. I know that. They are mammals. For them, like us, the gill apparatus gives way to an internal ear, to a complex auditory system. The tail, of course, does not recede into a sensitive mound of bone. Whale calves are born tail first into the world.

At eight weeks, there would have been no telling.

At home that evening, you ran me a bath. You added the purple bath beads you'd given me for Christmas, and the translucent globes melted into lavender oil beneath my toes. You rubbed my neck and shoulders. Sorry, you said, because you could never get the smell of engine oil out of your fingers. You brought me a glass of red wine to drink in the tub; you said it would be good for my iron levels. You stood at the side of the bath and, as I stepped out, dizzy with the heat and wine, you wrapped me in a towel and your arms. You took me on your lap and dried me like a child.

Nothing had come between us, after all.

Later, as I stood combing out my hair, you called from the porch. 'Helen, come see this.' Your voice was a net, hauling me back into the world. I threw the comb on to the dresser and pulled on my winter robe and old tennis shoes. Outside, you stood, your face turned towards the night sky. 'Switch off the light,' you said as I closed the kitchen door, and suddenly in the absolute darkness I lost you. 'Mike?'

'Over here,' you called. 'I'm over here.'

I edged my way down the four wooden stairs, gripping the thin banister, afraid to let go and worrying: about my half-tied laces, my head still wet in the frosty spring night, and the night itself, like the overturned keel of some broad-bottomed boat, trapping me beneath. Why had you made me switch off the light?

Then a rock reared up underfoot, and I was flying headlong. Your arm caught mine before I hit the ground. 'I'm here,' you said. 'I'm right here.'

I pressed my fingers to my eyes, pushing back tears.

'Relax,' you said. 'It's all right.'

'I can't get warm.'

You pulled me close to the heat of your chest. 'Look,' and I followed the pale line of your arm.

I nodded. 'A shooting star.' But it felt as far away as it actually was.

'And over there – another. And up there too. See? It's a meteor shower.'

I could hardly focus.

'Your folks won't be seeing this in the city tonight, I can tell you that. The lights will drown out everything.'

We stood in the unpaved driveway, between the stunted pine and spruce, and stared south-east at the unending sky. Over the hum of the generator, you counted one star after another as they reeled across the sky. 'Make a wish,' you said and you kissed the top of my head. 'Go on. Make a dozen wishes. I want you to have everything, Helen. I want you to have everything you want.'

'And what's that exactly?' I said, my voice strange in my throat.

Your arms fell away from me. I could smell the red wine on your breath as you struggled for words. 'I'm a mechanic, Helen.' I could almost see the punched-in confusion of your face. 'I'm not a god-damned mind-reader,' and you strode back to the house, kicking any rock or root in your path.

I stood, waiting for the light at the kitchen or bathroom window to guide me back in, but you found your way to bed, as oblivious as a blind man to the dark.

I left before you woke. I waited for the foghorn to sound as I closed the door behind me. I crossed the road and walked past your dad's deserted garage, past the post office, the gas station, the tiny graveyard where your mother was buried, Eileen's bakery, and the one-room library where my Bookmobile teetered on the curb. I turned at Moody's Store and took the path through the woods down to the beach, kicking off my shoes as my feet hit seagrass and sand.

The foghorn was still alive at the mouth of the Bay, mouthing its loneliness. The islands in the Bay – three hundred and sixty-five of them in all, one for every day of the year, they say out here – were still shrouded in fog and, maybe because of that, it seemed as if the day too had disappeared, as if calendar-time had been erased. It was June the 1st. Not possible. Our third anniversary.

I stripped down to my bra and underwear, and waded into the surf. My bones seized up as the cold shot through to my marrow, and I spluttered for air. It would be weeks still before the water was warm enough for tourists. Something skimmed my thigh and I flinched – a jellyfish, like a torn-out heart in the water beside me. I turned from it as a wave hit me in the chest, cutting my breath in two. But I stayed, afraid to go deeper, afraid to turn back. And I watched. As the sun burned off the morning fog. As the horizon asserted itself. As my legs lost all feeling. I watched, scanning the Bay for the flash of a dorsal fin or the fleeting arc of a back.

At this time of year, there were pods of pilot whales at the mouth of the Bay, some in families of a hundred or more. The Bay was a perfect echo chamber. A dolphin or whale could read the whole of its breadth in sonar clicks within moments.

I remembered the British scientist on the CBC as I'd sat that day dazed on the toilet, unable to flush it, unable to look again at the clots that had slipped from me. The voices from the kitchen radio reached me as if through some faulty satellite link, time-delayed. Nothing seemed real. He was saying that most of our DNA is actually obsolete; that it's composed largely of sequences of dead genes – for the fins we once had, for webbed feet, for a tail that had thrashed.

Three hundred millennia on, our blood is mainly, stubbornly, salt water. Yet at the age of thirty-one, I still couldn't swim. I stood there in the rising tide, ridiculous in my underwear, my legs turning waxen-white with the cold. At home, in our bed, as you reached for me, I lost my footing in the sand. As you threw back the quilt, calling my name, a wave rolled over my head.

Panic. Seaweed in my face. Water in my nose, in my lungs.

This was madness.

I stumbled from the surf choking, while a woman in a navy pea-jacket with a Labrador looked on, bemused.

I dressed, quickly. I walked, dripping, the way I'd come. I pretended I didn't see Donny Mullane watching me from behind the wheel of the school bus as he let the engine run. I nodded to your father as I passed the garage. He was hauling back the huge rattling doors, but you were nowhere in sight. He shouted something after me, but I only raised a hand.

I saw you before you saw me. You were hacking away at the saplings that colonized the driveway, cursing the roots that wouldn't come free. The forest was always closing in on us, like the ocean over the wake of a boat. You were only half-dressed. Where the hell had I been? Why was I wet? Did I realize you were about to phone the RCMP? Did I remember what day today was? Mrs Dempster at the library had already phoned. Well, she wasn't at the library yet. She was still getting her kids off to school, and did I know the Bookmobile was illegally parked?

I nodded.

You looked at me, seeing me properly at last. Why in God's name was I wet?

''Fraidy cat!' you used to shout, laughing when I wouldn't go into the water past my knees. 'Hold tight,' you'd say as I climbed on to your back in the surf, even though I was scared you might lose your footing in the sand, or get knocked by a sudden wave, but I thought, yes, I can do this. At least I can do this. I can hold on to your shoulders if you want me to. I can not let go. It was all you asked of me. It was all you seemed to need.

I took the axe from your hands and let it drop to the ground. I put my arms around you.

'You're wet,' you murmured.

'It's warm. I'll dry in no time.' It was early still. I stood cold and wet under the pearly June sky, and you were moved by the nearness of me, by my sudden openness to you, and you kissed me, pressing your lips to my cheek, to my lips; tasting the salt on my skin.

'Why?'

I shrugged.

'Did you fall in?'

'No.'

'What then?'

'Aren't you going to work today? Your dad's already –'

Under the palms of my hands, your spine stiffened. 'Christ Jesus.'

'I was just saying.'

'You tried to –'

'No. No, I swear.'

'It's the baby.'

'What is?'

'My God –'

'I didn't!'

'Who hauled you out?'

'It's not the baby.'

'Who?'

'No one hauled me out. I was just being . . . stupid.'

'Stupid? You can't even swim. That's not stupid. That's mental!'

I shrugged and looked past you.

'Who was down there?'

'I don't know . . .'

'Who?'

'I think it was Anna MacIntyre's mother-in-law.'

'She saw you?'

'Does it matter?'

'Christ Jesus.'

'What does it matter?'

'Do you have any idea how much people whisper around here? Do you want to fit in or don't you?'

'The phone's ringing.'

'Let it.'

'It might be –'

'Forget the phone. I'm talking to you.'

'I can't think with it –'

I pushed you away, but you got to the door ahead of me and almost pulled it off the wall as you answered. 'Yup . . . Now . . . ?' Your eyes were still bleary. '*Jesus.*' The day's blood hadn't come into your face yet. 'Sure I've got rope, but Christ, Tom, rope? You'll need a friggin' JCB.' Your shoulders were growing rounded. Your chest seemed to be sinking these days.

You pulled on a grimy T-shirt as I followed you to the door. 'What is it? What's happened?'

'We're going to sort this out when I get back. Okay? Go dry your hair and get out of those clothes. And call the library. They want to know if you're coming in or not.'

There were no major shipping lanes near the Bay. No oil tankers. No industrial noise.

It was a mature male pilot whale. Thirteen feet long. He'd swum in too close and beached himself.

Our hamlet had a population of just sixty-two, including the children. Far too few to shift an estimated 1,800 pounds. The Oceanographic Institute had been contacted. They were sending people, equipment. Local fishermen were put on alert. Other pilot whales might follow. That's what the marine biologist on the phone said. Pilot whales have strong family bonds. Mass strandings are not uncommon. If necessary, the pods would have to be herded and hounded back to the mouth of the Bay. Or we'd risk a mass grave on the beach.

I crossed the road for the third time that day, and walked past the garage, the post office and the library. I took the sandy path through the woods and on to the beach. As I arrived, you looked up, angry still behind the huge fluked tail.

I avoided you and joined the makeshift team who were bucketing water from the Bay over the whale's black flanks. Johnny Flynn was pointing out the squid sucker marks and tooth scars on him. I edged up the line, past the elbowed flippers, and when no one was looking I stroked the bulbous round of his forehead, smooth except for a few encrusted barnacles. His blowhole was the size of my palm. His eyes were shut, their huge lids fluttering beneath the markings of two pale white stripes. A biologist kept checking his watch. He recorded six minutes of sleep. REM sleep, he said. The whale was dreaming.

The haulage equipment never arrived. The director of tourism for the region did; there were implications for the summer season, he said. I gave up the vigil as the boats dropped anchor. I couldn't watch. 'Slow suffocation.' I'd heard the biologist mumble the words into his cellphone. 'God knows what took him in this close.'

You said it took three Cape Islanders and a mile of steel cable to shift him from the beach; that it was hard for the boats to get up to speed. You said he turned belly-up as he was pulled beyond the shallows, exposing – 'You won't believe it' – his penis, unsheathed and huge. I did believe it. I could see it in my mind's eye, quivering like the needle of some vast compass.

You hadn't noticed my bags in the hall. When you did, your face went pale as a leaf turned in a gale. 'What's going on?'

'Would you take me to the bus?'

'What for?'

'I'll phone you when I get there.'

'Your parents? Something wrong?'

'No, they're fine.'

'Well then, let's talk about it tomorrow. Let's go out tonight instead. Somewhere nice.'

'The bus is at four-thirty. I'm all packed, Mike.'

'Hold on a bit longer, eh? I'll take you tomorrow if you still want to go. I'll drive you in myself if that's what you want.'

'It is.'

'Give it another night then.'

'I can't.'

'I don't get it. Helen, I don't get what's going on.' You ran the back of your hand across your nose.

'It's just me. I'm not right.'

You sank on to your haunches. Your eyes were filling. 'I don't care. I love you however you are.'

'You shouldn't.'

'What the hell's that supposed to mean?' You started cracking your knuckles, tugging on your fingers as if you'd pull them from their joints.

'You deserve more. You deserve more from me.'

'Bullshit.'

'Okay.' I struggled to release the pull-handle on my big case. 'Then I deserve more – from me.'

'You going all women's lib on me, for God's sake? Women don't do that these days, Helen. It's not like I don't want you to do what you want to do. You want to see a man break down for you? Is that what all this is about? Well, okay, you've fucking got it, Helen. You've fucking got it.'

I'd never seen or heard you cry, and for a moment the strangeness of it, the choked-up rawness of it, frightened me more than the idea of the lonely bus ride ahead. You hadn't even cried when your mother died – not as she turned yellow with jaundice on her deathbed, not when she was lowered into the half-frozen ground of early April – but as you crouched there by the back door, you were suddenly sobbing and retching and sucking up air, ugly and broken and beloved with grief.

This much I can tell you. I miss the bite of the sea air. And the trance of the surf. And the cry of the foghorn. My windows rattle when the morning traffic starts, and I wake nervous without knowing why.

My apartment is across the street from the Y. It's small, basic, but it's enough. Muffled voices come through my walls. Sometimes the smell of cigarettes too. And footsteps overhead, as if someone else's life has been superimposed on mine; as if their step in this world is more sure, more substantial, than mine. But in time you can learn not to notice a lot.

I have lessons on Sundays. My swimsuit is aquamarine – a Lycra one-piece because it's streamlined in the water. I tuck my hair into a silicon cap. I wear goggles. My skin is turning scaly, in spite of all the moisturizer I slap on afterwards.

I'm actually getting good at breaststroke. I'm at intermediate level already. I thrash my feet hard as I glide forward – a 'whip-kick', it's called. Then, as my elbows come circling back, I bring them in close to my ribs and bob up in the water, 'undulating', my instructor says. It's what dolphins do, he says.

I have learned how to take long, powerful strokes, the cold water sluicing down my spine. Why do they call it 'crawl'? It's a lot better than that. I roll lightly on to a shoulder and hip when my lungs shout for air. I breathe deeply and dive, travelling alone at the very bottom of that small inland sea. I even somersault at the end of a length so my feet don't touch the floor of the pool.

You'd hardly know me.

Sometimes I think I will swim on and on for ever, the rhythm of the lengths and flips lulling me, length after length after length. Sometimes I almost think I'll get all the way to the Bay.

Discharge

When my wife, Angelina, is aroused, ball lightning slides from between her legs: a sphere of plasma, sometimes the size of an orange, sometimes the size of a basketball. Usually it is reddish-orange. Sometimes fluorescent white. More rarely still, that glowing green you see in pictures of the borealis.

We can feel the heat of it as it passes over our naked bodies, a small swift-moving sun. It rolls through the house, setting off overhead lights, my electric toothbrush, the breadmaker, the toaster, the juicer, the Moulinex, the TV, the computer, before finally settling under the dining-room table like an intransigent child. We know the behaviour.

In the bedroom, we stare at the ceiling, listening to the air pop in its wake, like the 'poof' of a dozen magnesium flashbulbs. The dog will start to bark – we no longer call to him. The doorbell might ring intermittently. The microwave will bleep.

You think I exaggerate.

You can pull the plug of a lamp from the socket, and the lamp will continue to shine. You can watch the digits on the stove clock spin. Later of course we'll find the fuses are blown, but no circuit breakers are tripped. The phone lines aren't down. There are no scorch marks.

On occasion, we have known it to pass through windows, storm windows too, a trembling globe that nestles deep within the bushes outside the house. Once, only the once, I saw it keep pace with a car, steady outside the passenger window at forty miles per hour.

It pulsates, an observation that is consistent with reports of ball lightning. More remarkably, it seems to display a kind of primitive intelligence or curiosity – also consistent. We have seen it bounce, zip, float, skim surfaces, change direction and, seemingly, follow one of us or the other. Usually, it will dissolve into a light switch, an antenna or, sometimes, my power drill.

Of course we know that ball lightning is associated with atmospheric disturbance; with damaged pylons, turbines or utility poles; and, in a few reports, with the gases arising from swamps or landfill. I've done the research.

We know it is not typically associated with states of arousal.

We make love less and less.

David is afraid, though he won't say he is. He is afraid it's like sticking your finger in a socket. And perhaps it is. Sometimes he's okay with a condom, though he rolls it on to himself furtively, saying nothing. He doesn't want to have to say to me that rubber is non-conductive.

So we pretend it will go away; that it will simply stop, like a minor venereal infection. And each time I think, there, it is gone from me. Gone, like that unfathomable baby in the bubble, free-floating at the end of *Space Odyssey*. Expelled. And I feel relieved. I can hear David saying, 'You're cold. Your skin's gone so cold,' and he's piling the duvet over me as I watch a small white sun orbit his left shoulder.

He prefers me cold. It's safer, after all.

At the Family Planning Clinic, I try to describe it. I try to be offhand. I say I feel like one of those statues that weeps tears – it can't be happening. The nurse humours me. She gives me a leaflet and a card with the address and opening hours of a discreetly named clinic. She says my partner or partners will also have to be treated. She says it shouldn't affect my fertility if it is caught early. She recommends cotton gussets.

David started as an assessor at a small insurance firm in the eighties and branched out into Risk Assessment in '94. It was a smart move. Network monitoring. Security management. System-audit investigation. Surveillance. Environmental-hazard estimates. Nothing, he will tell you with a grin, is without risk – it is merely a case of making people feel it.

He merged with another consultancy in '99, and the company has grown exponentially. He and Walter get calls now from the UK, Australia, Brazil. They say there's no telling what a day will bring. From Japan yesterday it was a case of data protection – standard, except they wanted the figures to represent the threat posed not only by viruses, worms and the latest spyware, but also by 'zombie computers' and 'swarm intelligence'. In Dallas last month it was more probability flow charts for bio-terror. In Montana last week it was a Men's Liberation Group wanting projections on the threat to male reproduction 'in light of residual oestrogens and the new cloning technologies'.

Walter and David didn't take the Montana case, of course. But David wasn't laughing it off either. He was remembering how all the cloning stuff started with sheep eggs in Scotland; how an electrical pulse and not a sperm activated the development of the embryo. And for a moment, as he talked between mouthfuls of smoked meat on rye, he studied me.

No information, he says, is trivial. No event is outside the net of risk methodology. Everything is Threat, Vulnerability, Control or Attack. He's got 3-D relational models in moulded plastic that balance on his desk, and animated, interactive versions on DVD for the client to watch at home at their own convenience. Threat is black. Vulnerability is yellow. Control is blue. Attack is red. When I ask him if he isn't simply peddling paranoia, he smiles oddly and tells me it pays to be paranoid.

Soon he will have an affair. He will have an affair to punish me. Because he cannot see that he is the source of the secret charge that lies at the centre of me.

*

Angelina is laughing at her white-wine sauce. Spoiled. And the fish is overdone. Walter and Kate have arrived over an hour late for dinner. A four-car pile-up off exit 10.

Kate is laden with apologies and chrysanthemums. Walter glowers over the drink I slide into his hand. It's obvious they've argued – always more risky in a car because there's little eye contact, so you're bound to be less human to one another. I take the situation in hand. I call, book a table. 'What do we tell our clients, Walter?' I say. 'Plan on Plan B.' Walter forces a laugh.

'David, you promised,' Angelina says, grabbing my hand.

I smile broadly. 'I did: Walter, work is officially out of bounds tonight.'

'Or else,' and she winks at Kate. I don't release her hand.

We show our guests through the kitchen and on to the deck. The evening is bright. The drone of random lawnmowers drugs us fleetingly. We listen to the receding calls of kids on the street, spectral as radio waves in space.

'A drink, ladies?' I offer.

Back in the kitchen, I chop limes, scoop chopped ice, and mix spritzers in tall frosted glasses. 'You might as well relax out there,' I call through the screen door. 'We've got an hour till the reservation.'

'Great,' I hear Kate say as she leans back into a lounger. 'The garden's looking wonderful, Angelina. Are those hollyhocks over there?'

'Yes, incredible, aren't they? I sketched a sort of plan when we moved in, one for each bed. But the soil's so acidic it seems miraculous to me every time something actually grows.'

'Angelina's the brains around here,' I say, emerging, hands full, 'and I, as you can see, am the brawn.'

Angelina smiles, rolls her eyes, and takes the tray from my arms. 'Dip, Walter?'

'Thanks. In our case, Kate's the brawn, and I'm just obedient.'

'Kate, dip?'

'If only you were, honeybun.' Kate helps herself to smoky cheese flavour.

We play married couples. We mock-fight to give the illusion that we are not fighting. We banter to show sexual spark. Walter, I notice, has given up flirting with Angelina. At one time, it was flattery when she appeared in the office; jokey repartee on the phone; womanly advice gratefully received. Now nothing. A sign not only that his wife is in the room, but also, in all likelihood, an indication that Walter, after six years of business partnership, fears he is actually in love with my wife.

Our spaniel, Perry Mason – Perry to family – finishes his bowl of Pedigree Chunks and runs on to the deck, eager for attention. Kate and Angelina fuss, oblivious to canine drool and Dr Ballard's Pedigree breath. Walter throws Perry's red rubber ball, and the pooch bounds into the backyard, straight across Angelina's alpine rock garden. I survey the evening. Walter and Kate are still not speaking. Angelina and Kate are awkward outside the clockwork of a four-course meal. Walter and I are not permitted to talk about work and are busy feigning equanimity. Angelina and I pretend that we are as always.

We are two childless couples without the white noise of birth weights, school antics and orthodontistry to lull us into a sense of intimacy.

'David,' Walter begins, red ball once more in hand, 'in case I forget to mention it tomorrow, I sent a copy of that consultative report for Boeing to – Oops.' He looks at Angelina with a sheepish smile. 'That's one demerit for me, I guess.'

'Afraid so,' Angelina says with a tssk of her tongue. 'Which means we need a forfeit for Walter.' She puts down her glass and claps her hands. He laughs. I watch Kate watching Walter, who can't take his eyes off Angelina. 'Okay. I've got it. What do you think, Kate? For being so dull, Walter has to regale us with . . . with a good true-life story or an amazing fact. Something none of us knows.'

'David,' says Walter with a grin, 'I don't recall you warning me about your wife.'

I shrug, a seemingly helpless man.

Angelina alights from her wicker chair, runs into the house, and returns with a plastic egg-timer and one of my golf gloves. 'And listen carefully, Walter,' she instructs, 'if anyone does know the story or fact already, you lose and we up the ammo.'

'Which means?'

'Which means . . .' She thinks, her finger pressed to her lip. 'We'll want a confession out of you next.'

'Can I call my lawyer first?'

'You could, honey,' says Kate, fingering the rim of her glass, 'if you hadn't tried to sue him last year.'

Walter ignores her. 'Okay, but one thing, Angelina. If none of you does know it – and clearly we're operating on the trust system here – that's game over, right?'

'And pass up your chance for revenge? Now where's the fun in that? Noooo. You get to throw down the golf glove to any one of us, Walter. Same terms.'

'What time did you say that table was ready, David?'

'On your mark, Walter. Get set. Your time begins – NOW.'

Walter doubles up in his chair, resting his head between his knees, like a winded man. Kate and I exchange smiles while Angelina watches the sand in the timer trickle away.

'Beeeeep! Right, Walter. That's your time up.'

'Okay. Um, this is the only amazing fact that comes to mind. Well, it amazed me. In London, one of the bridges that spans the Thames is Blackfriars Bridge. And, apparently, it was considered quite a good one to kill yourself from, don't ask me why. Anyway, I don't know what colour this particular bridge was, but they decided to paint the whole thing green, and guess what?'

'Laura Ashley objected,' says Kate.

I tip my glass to her, conspiratorially. She passes me hers for a top-up, our fingertips touching briefly.

Angelina is not distracted. 'What happened, Walter?'

'The suicide rate, the rate of jumps that is, dropped by 34 per cent.'

'Really? Wow. And because of such a simple thing as green paint.' Angelina is looking at Walter like he is the Buddha in a viscose jacket and bad tie.

I'm impatient with the game. 'Your turn, Walter,' I remind him. 'Go on.' He picks up the golf glove and, thinking it rude to throw it at either his host or hostess, throws it instead at his wife's feet.

'Not fair,' she pouts.

Angelina picks up the egg-timer. 'Ready, Kate? Ready? Go!'

Kate has that feature particular to some women who have reached the age of forty. Her chin is tipped eternally upward so that her face seems to float, owl-like, without reference to her neck. 'Right. Here goes. Amazing fact: the clitoris has over eight thousand nerve endings. More than twice as many as the penis.'

'God love it,' I venture.

'He'd better because He's the only one who's going to find it,' Walter snorts.

'Sorry, Kate. I knew that,' Angelina admits. 'There was a programme on the Discovery Channel last week, wasn't there?'

'Confession time,' says Walter. 'Confess, my darling. That's the rule.'

Kate stabs the lime at the bottom of her glass with her stir-stick. 'So who died and made Walter God?'

'Give me that thing, Angelina,' and Walter turns over the egg-timer, jubilant. 'The clock's running, Kate. Confess.'

'What do you know?' she says, almost immediately. 'I've suddenly thought of something. Firstly, Walter and I fought all the way here. Secondly, he's been a complete bastard for – gosh, how long has it been, honey? Six months? A year?'

Walter doesn't falter. 'Now, darling, as Angelina already

explained, you have to tell them something they *don't* already know.'

'Of course. Sorry. I forgot.' She takes a sip from her glass. 'I'm pregnant.'

'Something true, Kate. Or something credible at the very least.'

'We're having a baby.'

'We are not having a baby.'

She roots in the oversized bag at her feet and passes Walter a small cardboard envelope. The label's big, in bold-faced caps. Difficult not to see. NUCHAL TRANSLUCENCY ULTRASOUND SCAN (11 WEEKS).

The egg-timer cracks between his thumb and forefinger. A thin stream of golden sand spills like urine on to his shoes.

But I'm watching Angelina. I'm watching Angelina who's staring helplessly at Walter. And in that moment I see it all. I see in her wild stare the sudden carelessness of someone who's been overwhelmed by circumstances. Betrayed. I see he told her he was no longer sleeping with Kate, that the marriage was stale. I see Angelina loves him.

And I say nothing. My heart is a blister, but I say nothing.

David watches me, but will not look at me. I say, 'What is it? What have I done?' and he says, 'That's interesting. Why do you think you've done anything?' His pupils have contracted to almost nothing, as if he's disappearing from even himself.

Sometimes, we walk out in the early evenings, before dark, and the streetlights flicker into life as I pass, one after another, as if the charge inside me is getting bigger. And, as we walk, lost to our own thoughts, I see David smile to himself, as if my growing energy confirms some wordless suspicion.

In the stillness of our bed, he no longer touches me.

Kate's decided to continue with the pregnancy. She's forty-four, but she says that's nothing these days. She's traded the cocktail hour for yoga after work with a backpacker just back from Bali. She persuades me to go shopping online with her for maternity wear. She tells me she wants to flaunt rather than flatter; that she plans to look like an ancient fertility figure in Lycra and office neutrals. Walter appears pleased – their last chance, he jokes, to make it in the suburban family jungle.

Kate doesn't know that I know; even David doesn't know that Walter was sterilized three years ago. I say nothing to Walter – I pretend I never knew – and I know he is grateful.

I do not even ask myself who the father is.

Last week, David and I were eating dinner – a beef stew I'd had in the freezer for months. The evening news was still on in the other room. Neither of us got up to turn it off. Inertia settled between us like fog. Perry kept vigil under the table at our feet, begging as always for scraps. David said not to, but as I chewed, I bent down to slip him a chunk of meat and, as I did so, I started to choke. David passed me my glass of water but I waved it away. I couldn't drink for coughing. So he threw down his napkin, pushed back his chair, and started clapping me on the back. My eyes were watering. Perry gazed up at me. I wanted to say, stop, stop, afraid David would lodge it deeper within me, afraid he'd kill me for my own good, but I couldn't breathe to speak. He pounded my back harder. The broad beat of his hand sounded in my lungs. I thought I felt something crack, a rib, an airway, I couldn't tell. David was pulling up my blouse, unfastening the clip of my bra. I felt his arms encircle me, rigid and primed for action. My eyes strained in their sockets. Perry wagged his tail. And suddenly, before the deadlock of David's arms tensed around me, something rose in my throat and filled my mouth.

Perry started to bark and thump his tail noisily, as if I were beckoning him in some game, and, I thought, it can't be. How can it be? How can Perry's rubber ball be in my mouth? My jaws were locking around it. My lungs still burned. David was about to call 911 when I finally managed to spit it into my hands.

It wasn't Perry's ball. It was no ragged chunk of meat. It was a red plasmic orb that hovered, delicate and trembling, over the cup of my palms. My eyes streamed as I beheld it: a small blood-orange of a sun, bright and angry as a newborn's head.

Each day it grows.

Coupling

In the dark of the tent, against the blare of the footlights, I couldn't see who had done it. I couldn't see anyone at all, except Won, our Taiwanese dwarf, selling fortune cookies to someone in the front row. A smashed candy-apple lay at my feet. The gob of spit was running down my cheek into my beard. I couldn't move. My cue came again. Someone coughed. The canvas of the tent snapped with a vengeance in the wind. Then, blackout.

I felt an arm on my shoulders, fingers tracing small circles on my back, on my neck. We walked into the wings.

Lucie lifted a hand and wiped my face and beard with a crumpled tissue. I knew the slim fingers, their tips nicotine-yellow. I knew the twisting serpent ring and its gold-plate flash. I started to breathe easier. A tech-man was beside us, behind us, shifting props in a sweat. The stage manager was shouting down his earpiece. He tripped over a fibreglass ring of Saturn and swore; noticed me and swore again.

'Come on,' Lucie said.

The afternoon light was strange, mercurial, after the brittle darkness of showtime. Clusters of people idled outside. Children peeked under billowing tent flaps. Ticket stubs, stray balloon-dogs and greasy burger wrappers blew on a wind already littered with the lost chances of Won's paper fortunes. Lucie staggered after one thin strip, trapped it clumsily underfoot, then unfolded it, triumphant. 'YOU WILL TAKE A VIRILE LOVER. Well.'

I said nothing.

We stumbled over guy-ropes and prostrate children. Behind us, the show tent grew smaller and smaller, and the pink stream of discarded cotton candy ran dry. Ahead, the main road stretched into town. Suddenly I wanted to go back. I said, 'Your feet. It's too far. It's at least three miles.'

Lucie looked at me. 'Did I or did I not run away and join the circus?'

'My bet is you didn't actually run.'

'You're right. I sauntered. I have always managed a certain style, and a place called Hunckton is not about to change that. Are you coming or aren't you?'

The day was damp, unpromising. The town was small. Too small. I felt like Houdini, clambering for the airlock inside the canister of milk. WELCOME TO HUNCKTON, the sign read, HOME-TOWN OF MISS AMERICA 1967. I could see it all: the Main Street homecoming parade, the gleaming convertible Chevrolet, the white-gloved wave, her poised perch atop the back seat, the shining poof of her chestnut hair, the bannered breast, the maiden cheek.

The green light at the crosswalk was blinking WALK – WALK–WALK. Lucie lurched on to the crosswalk. I stared at the black blocks that passed for shoes on those sad club feet.

I had grown up in a town like this back in New Brunswick, a place none of my fellow carnies had ever heard of. A Canadian province, I'd say. North of Maine, I'd explain, and they'd laugh and say how could there be anything north of Maine? Where was I really from?

I'd escaped ten years ago, the year before I finished high school, but a decade on the look of Hunckton's Main Street was still all too familiar. It was a street with ageing mannequins in yesteryear fashion in every shopfront; a street where frustrated adolescents took turns humping the one pinball machine in town. It was a place where the Christmas lights never came down; where year in, year out, you lived under the unlit absurdity of a Santa's sleigh or a burned-out Star of Bethlehem; where, come good weather, fly-swatters helped pass the time.

I kept my head down.

So I'm not sure how long it was before I'd noticed Lucie was gone. Vanished.

I moved down the street, past a liquor store and the Good News Bible Bookstore; past the funeral home that boasted a 'caring lady undertaker'; past the dark tobacco shop, empty but for the sound of a ghostly TV ballgame, and the pet shop with a listless snake in its window front.

A bell rang as I entered In-Step Shoes, begrudgingly. 'For God's sake, what are you doing in here of all places?'

'Browsing.'

'For what?'

'What does it look like?'

'You're buying *shoes*?'

'Who knows? It's like I said. I'm browsing.'

'For Hushpuppies, fake-leather golf shoes or the saddle shoes they didn't manage to sell in 1958?'

'*Now* you're talking.'

'Come on. Before someone mistakes you for normal.'

But Lucie was seated now, legs stubbornly crossed and one foot swinging like a crazy pendulum between us. A thin young woman in a beige A-line skirt approached. 'Can I help you?' she said to Lucie.

'I certainly hope so. I'm looking for something cooler for summer. Maybe a sandal. Ideally something that doesn't involve a lace-up sock.'

She looked at Lucie's custom-made blocks and gulped. 'Do you happen to know, um, what size you take?'

'Now that's a good question. Should I call my orthopaedist?'

'No.' She twisted the end of her long, wispy ponytail. 'I mean, that's okay. I'll get the measuring plate.'

When she reappeared, Lucie's feet were bare. 'Don't worry about this lump of skin here. Just think of it as my heel.'

The three of us stared at the misshapen stumps. 'Um, I'm new here.' She looked at me, then looked away. 'If you don't mind waiting, I'll just go find the manager.'

I grabbed the blocks that called themselves shoes, shoved Lucie's feet in, laced up the socks, hooked the braces, and got us out of the shop. I could feel the hot beat of my blood in my neck.

'*That*,' said Lucie, 'was rude.'

I winced. It was rude. I didn't know what to say.

'The poor girl will be wondering where we got to.'

I grinned, relieved. 'She'll get over it.' Next door, outside the drugstore, two teenagers emerged from a photo booth and dawdled by the slot, waiting for their celluloid testament to young love.

'Us next,' Lucie announced as the machine rattled and whirred.

The girl checked her cellphone for messages. The boy buried his face in her neck, sucking away on her candy-heart necklace. At last, the photos dropped.

'I thought they'd never leave,' said Lucie. 'What colour background do you want?'

'Tell me why we're doing this,' but I allowed myself to be pushed on to the stool.

'Something to remember the day by.'

I raised my jacket collar. 'As if I'm about to forget.'

When the first flash exploded in our faces, Lucie laughed, and I turned to stone.

'Do you think we could get my feet in the next shot? Give me a hand, quick.'

I stared at the stickers plastered to the walls. The Samaritans. A lost pet rabbit. Pole-Cats, a twenty-four-hour pole-dancing club. Under my elbow, I could just make out the card of a pre-op transsexual 'looking for redneck love'. Then the red eye turned green, and the second shot flashed like the ire of God.

'This is no good. We need drama. Kiss me.' And Lucie was on me with a mouth like a trick plunger.

As the third flash exploded, I flung back the curtain and started walking.

'Wait up! I just wanted –'

'Go to hell!' I shouted.

'I do. Six nights a week and Wednesday matinées!'

I walked as fast as I could – and straight into a fat kid coming out of the public library. His pencil case fell to the ground. A Magic Marker rolled towards me. We both reached for it, suddenly eye to eye. But before I could pass it to him, he was walking away at speed, head down.

At the outskirts of town, I could hear again the screams from the fair, a strange frequency on the breeze. I ducked into a bus shelter to hide. From nobody. Across the street, a couple of teenagers were mowing the lawns in the municipal cemetery. In another town, they would have been bronzed summer lifeguards or smiling fast-food employees on some Miracle Mile. But here, they were struggling with the right angles of the dead.

A bus pulled up, the Number 9, and Lucie got off. 'So what's the itinerary?'

I looked away.

'If I'd stayed on, apparently I could have seen the home of Miss America 1967.'

'You're a saddo,' I said but I made room on the shining metallic bench.

'Human anomaly, please. You have language. Use it.'

A picture of a bright-eyed stewardess smiled benevolently down from an airline ad. 'The day trip is over.'

'Over? We're just getting started.'

I got to my feet. 'I'll see you round.'

'Chicken shit.'

'What?' I said.

'Chicken-shit scared. As in: you are. And there's me thinking I had the vernacular right.'

I stuffed my hands into my pockets and started to walk. Then I felt the fat kid's marker loose among my change and turned.

Lucie was just about to light up. I approached the smiling stewardess. I removed the cap from the marker. The smell of its thick tip was delicious as I put the black nib to her glowing cheek.

That evening, the air was balmy. The wind had gone quiet, like a dog down and whimpering on a lean belly. The song of the outflow pipe into the river calmed me. I sat in my trailer, flipping through the previous week's TV guide. The techies were shouting to each other as the rides were dismantled. The tents collapsed with a whoosh. Martha, our octogenarian with three breasts who had been in the business since the days of the Dime Museums, waved as she passed my screen door with a cup of tea. I waved back but looked away again.

From somewhere, I could hear the digital notes of a snake-charmer's flute trembling on the air. Then came the sound of Lucie stumbling up my steps.

I concentrated on the TV blurbs. 'Made it back then.'

'Of course I made it back.'

I nodded but didn't look up.

'I liked the artwork.'

'Oh.' I turned a page. 'That.'

'How did you get up on the billboard?'

I shrugged.

'I thought Sarah Jessica Parker looked better, strangely. The beard suited her, even if she is otherwise blonde these days.'

'Thanks for coming by.'

A strip of pictures landed across my TV guide. One shot of the two of us. One mostly of me as Lucie dived footwards. The third of Lucie in profile, surprised, plus the blur of my shoulder and right arm. The fourth frame was blank.

I couldn't look at myself. But I couldn't not look at Lucie.

Beautiful. Lucent. Bright-eyed. Skin made for the flashbulb. A face that seemed to draw everything that was light into it.

I smiled, still not looking up. 'You could be a pretty young thing with that peachy face of yours.'

'Better the devil you know.'

'I'm not so sure.'

'Well you, you could be an old man with those droopy tits of yours. What have I told you? Sit up straight. Don't slouch. Take care of yourself, will you.'

I looked up, hurt, exposed. But Lucie was smiling, and I'd never before felt such warmth. 'You sound like Martha. She's always telling me.'

'And wouldn't *she* know? *Three* breasts. I ask you, wouldn't she know?'

I suppressed a smile.

'Now walk to the river with me.'

Won's green-and-orange Chinese lanterns floated over the bank. Fireflies glowed electric in the twilight. We were at the river's edge, leaning over the shallows, just catching our reflections in the darkening water. There was the yellow glimmer of Lucie's head, the white splash of my brow. But I was almost lost in that glassy darkness, my face obscured by the dark of my beard.

We took off our shoes and dangled our feet over the bank, kicking at the water, wanting to break up the quiet that had crept up on us out of nowhere. I was glad of the dark. It covered my face where that spit had been. It let Lucie's small twisted feet splash in the water. With those god-given hooves and a ten-volt tail, 'Lucifer: the Pretender' was cheap lightning on stage. My act, on the other hand, depended on little more than me, ridiculous in flounces and a sash.

'They'll shut us down soon, you know,' I said. 'Could be any day.'

'Yes. Any day.'

'So why do you stick with this?'

'Because I never could get to fifth position in ballet class.'

'I'm serious,' I said.

'So am I. Have you ever *been* to private school?'

On the ground beside me, a firefly crept towards the bank. I tried to lure it into my palm, its tail flickering.

Lucie watched. 'You haven't said why you're here.'

'You tell me,' I said, still concentrating. 'Because there's no business like show business? Because Springer hasn't phoned yet? Because, deep down, I'm afraid I have a weak chin?'

'You don't trust me.'

'Not much,' I said.

'I'd worry of course if you did.'

'I know that.'

We smiled. In the half-light of the lanterns, I was fixed by those eyes, wide as the river, wide as the night. My hand moved to Lucie's thigh. Lean, muscular. Something passed, a current, between us. For the first time, in that moment, I felt mutable.

Then his cheek brushed mine, and he was over me, running his fingers over my breasts, across my face.

Notes for a Chaotic Century

The thing is this. In a non-linear or chaotic system, feedback can exceed input. Which means you might well get more than you bargained for. And then a lot more again.

Branch manager John Monaghan can only repeat what has already been said: 'We are very, very sorry. We're overwhelmed by what's happened.' He blinks several times in the light of the new day. He confirms that the branch will not recommence trading until five that afternoon. He adds that, given the events of last night, all opening offers have been withdrawn. Irrationally, he wishes he hadn't left Daisy, his youngest daughter, at her nursery – he suddenly feels the need for her small, plump hand in his. The reporters are out, even at this early hour, and his Adam's apple is bobbing like an Ikea ball in the ball pit of his throat.

The company blames an unforeseen volume of customers. An anticipated one thousand shoppers swelled to six thousand by midnight, even before the doors for the new flagship store were opened. In the chaos that ensued, twenty-two people were treated for heat exhaustion and crush injuries. A man was stabbed in Ikea's car park – in an alleged fight over a parking space. Ambulances were delayed by unprecedented congestion on the A406 as people abandoned their cars and made their way to the store on foot in a new, twenty-first-century pilgrimage. 'We could not have predicted the numbers,' John Monaghan repeats under a volley of questions.

And it's true. As any chaotician will tell you, in the state of chaos, only change is predictable.

Not that chaos is random. On the contrary, it follows rules so delicate they often escape human measure. It gives way to patterns so intricate, they quickly exceed our grasp – as in the growth of a snowflake, or a forest, or a forest fire, or a stock market, or a cancer in the body. As in the action of a whirlpool at a kitchen drain, or an eddy in a river, or road traffic on the M25, or the rapid-fire of thought in the brain.

That said, you could certainly be forgiven for mistaking the 'chaotic' for mayhem. You could be forgiven along with John Monaghan, who is at a loss to provide the reporters with answers; along with security guard Gerard Vincent, whose jaw was dislocated when he was punched by an irate shopper in soft furnishings; along with fifty-year-old Anna Lanchester, who was wrestled to the checkout floor by three younger women before they seized her flatbed trolley and purchased her cut-price, leather three-seater sofa.

The non-linear system is unimaginably sensitive to initial conditions – to the smallest, the manifold and the least discernible of inputs. The devil, as they say, is in the detail.

Nick stands at his North London window and watches passing trains, bright vertebrae of light in the midwinter dark. It is not yet dinner time and already he finds himself worrying about the insomnia of the night to come. At three, maybe four in the morning, he'll give up on sleep, switch on the desk lamp by the cracked lounge window, and try as usual to turn his attention to his tentative master's thesis.

It has yet to take on the critical mass it needs to survive. His field is cultural anthropology; his subject, the female fertility figure. The survey begins, unsurprisingly, with the prehistoric Venus of Willendorf in all her corpulent abundance. Nick goes on to explore the Celtic Sheela-na-gig, she of the splayed vulva. Procreative icon or cautionary crone? He will go on to ask what happened to the female fertility figure in the industrial age. He will examine Jacob Epstein's sculpture *Maternity* in all its elemental force, and Picasso's ample *Nude Woman with a Necklace*, from between whose parted legs a river surges.

The dissertation will offer, Nick feels sure, a new slant on the fertility dolls of Ghana. It will examine the ostensibly biological foundations for the Western cult of the Barbie body, using new research which suggests that levels of two hormones vital to fertility are indeed higher in women with big breasts and narrow waists – Nick has read the early papers out of Romso University. Finally, he will consider the role of the latest robot sex doll, which features large breasts and nipples as standard, and extra-large breasts and nipples for an extra-large price. She breathes fast and encouragingly during sex. Her body temperature rises. With the use of a remote control, she will wiggle her hips as she straddles you. You can even press your ear to her warm, silicon chest and hear the urgent beat of an electronic heart.

Tonight, for Nick, there is no solace. The advert he read on the tube earlier today repeats on him like a bad takeaway. 'Join us for Unbeatable Discounts at the Midnight Opening of our New Flagship Store. We have Dream Designs for Your Every Waking Moment.'

Nick has many waking moments. It feels as if he hasn't slept in a week. His eyes are cavernous. His skin is pasty. He worries his hair is falling out. By night, his only company are the trains that hurtle past like destiny at the dead-end of his road.

The truth is, he wouldn't mind a midnight opening. The company of other nocturnal wanderers. A bit of fanfare. Besides, he can't help but recall: there are more pregnant women per square foot in Ikea than in your average city hospital.

It is this final thought – and the subsequent dopamine rush to his brain – that dispels Nick's inertia, propelling him out the door and down the road in the direction of the next train departing from Tottenham Hale.

Allan, on the other hand, is already on the Number 192 bus. With any luck it should drop him within walking distance of the new yellow-and-blue, 300,000-square-foot blight on the North London horizon. McFurniture, he calls it. The only reason it's environmentally friendly, he tells himself, is because no trees go into the making of it. He read in the local paper that Ikea stores take up 3,979,600 square metres across the planet. He did the maths. That's the equivalent of 577 Premiership football pitches – minus the jubilation.

He toyed, briefly, with the idea of something he saw on the web. Furniture kits for divorced men. For £1,350 you were equipped with a living room, a complete bedroom, a dining room and a television set, including a DVD. Not bad, he'd thought. After all, three months had passed and he was still sleeping on an air mattress. He was still cooking on his old two-burner camp stove and eating off tin plates. In the end, he conceded Ikea would be easier. He used to accompany Julia, his ex, under duress, to the store in Brent Park, escaping to the food hall while she deliberated over swivel chairs, armchairs and swivel armchairs, as if their domestic equilibrium depended on it.

Maybe it did.

He's not sure about anything any more.

Except geography. Allan teaches geography at Aylward Comprehensive. Today, he gave up on the exports of the fifty American states and tried to teach the kids about geomagnetism instead. He explained that the earth itself is a magnet. No one knows, he said, exactly why, though the molten iron and nickel at its core have a lot to do with it. But unlike, say, your ordinary fridge magnet, the earth's magnetic fields aren't constant. There are fluctuations and surprises, especially when you factor in the sun's magnetic field. Because, on our favourite star, thermonuclear reactions bubble up from its core, showering us with streams of charged particles. So our local magnetic field interacts with these sun-charged particles to produce an even more sensitive electro-magnetism. 'Which means this lump of rock we call Earth,' he concluded, 'is anything but inanimate. You got me? It buzzes and it hums and it crackles.'

Which is when the bubble of pink chewing gum being blown by Kylie Nickerson (or 'Knickers-off', as the graffiti in the boys' toilet would have it) reached its maximum circumference and exploded with a resounding crack.

'Result,' declared 'Genghis Kahn' Kaleel from beneath his parka hood.

'Ta,' said Kylie.

Allan works out his frustrations playing five-a-side football with a community group twice a week. He's a strong voice behind their fund-raising efforts for a local youth centre and a strong voice against the group's decision to move to a field with astro-turf. He talks about the rate of injuries. He talks about the effects on ball control. He doesn't talk about the deep-in-his-gut feeling that contact with the ground is somehow important; that we have to keep our feet firmly planted; that maybe there's a line or current of energy we shouldn't be without.

As Allan alights from the bus, he wonders again about the mysteries of magnetism. It is not yet eight and already he can see a blinking tailback of cars on the North Circular Road. In the freshly paved car park, the queue of shoppers is already many, many rows deep.

He draws breath. Is he up to this? Julia always said he was colour blind. He is afraid he doesn't know how to put things together. Short of buying everything in one colour, he doesn't know how to make things match. Deep down, he is afraid he will never be able to make his new flat feel like a home. Deep down, he is afraid he will keep waking in the middle of the night – heart banging, spine rigid – not knowing where the hell he is.

Rachel and Aisling are exactly where they want to be. They've been queuing since seven. They missed the free hot drinks, but they're close enough to the front to enjoy the flame-throwers, stilt-walkers and the a-cappella group. Rachel is a registered community midwife who's waiting for the call from one of her overdue ladies. 'It'll be tonight. Mark my words.' She trusts her instincts as much as her training; has done ever since she was a girl, elbow-deep in ewes on her family's Wiltshire farm. 'There's no creature born with a greater will to die than a sheep,' she once told Aisling. 'Whereas babies' – she waved her hand – 'babies practically haul themselves into the world.' She tells Aisling she'd might as well be awake when the call comes, and what better way to pass the time than twenty-four-hour shopping?

Aisling is a senior staff oncology nurse, with special training in pain management. In her hospice, that means not only your standard opioid analgesics, but also, she makes sure, good beer and boxes of wine in the communal fridge, an abundance of chocolates, occasional packs of ciggies and a few top-shelf magazines for those in need. 'They're ill,' she declared at one staff meeting. 'They're not dead.' When Aisling speaks, people tend to listen.

She met Rachel at a Cuban salsa class at the local leisure centre. Typically, there weren't enough men, so they were paired up. Aisling agreed to lead; Rachel provided the rhythm. More than a year later, they still move as one. So when Rachel first saw the advert for discounted mattresses and the Noresund lacquered-steel double-bed frame, complete with metalwork motifs, she knew nothing else would do. When Aisling saw the price – thirty quid to the first 500 – she got the flask and the fold-up chairs.

There is every promise in a new double bed: warmth to be had, wine to be spilled, crumbs to be slept upon, and the ghosts of old lovers banished. Tonight, as the thousands gather, a fire-breather stops near Aisling and Rachel. He throws back his head, opens his mouth wide to the February night and exhales a sudden fury of flames. Yet Aisling turns not to him but to Rachel, for in the wild and smoking light, her face is bright, arresting, magnificent.

Not far behind, Bob and Imelda hold hands against the night. They're not used to being outside, under the sulphurous glow of the North London sky, among strangers as it nears midnight. Imelda feels unusually awake, as you do when you find yourself at night in another country. It's like that somehow, the Ikea car park. The familiarity of the moon and the stars takes her by surprise, as it did that first time they sat on the darkened terrace of their time-share in Spain all those years ago. In the morning, she remembers, the outdoor table and chairs were covered in a fine, red dust, and when a neighbour explained it was sand blown over from the Sahara, Imelda marvelled that a bit of Africa could be right there on her terrace; that the world could be so connected.

Bob suggested they come out tonight. 'We can just look,' he said. 'No harm looking, is there?' Last month, on his final cheque, he brought home a breadmaker and had refused to take it back. Not that she wasn't enjoying it; she was running the gamut. White bloomers. Wholewheat loaves. Malt bread. Raisin bread. Pesto-and-pine-nut bread. But both she knew and Bob knew. No amount of bread was going to fill the hole, the hole left when the boys moved out, all three within a year; the hole into which a large part of Imelda had slipped.

So the timing of Bob's redundancy could hardly have been worse. Not only were there university fees to pay, but the prospect of retirement in Spain was also looking ever more distant. And these days, Imelda couldn't think beyond the morning telly listings. Hadn't Bob always managed things? Hadn't he worked for over thirty years as a logistics manager for a major airline? In his time, he'd overseen shipments of everything: racing cars, racing horses, small yachts, a rare Asian elephant, paintings by Degas, Dutch flowers, De Beers diamonds, a polar bear, a prehistoric alpine man, twenty thousand kilos of asparagus, zoo animals, live lobsters, and lead-lined coffins. 'Life,' he once told Imelda with a laugh, 'is cargo. It's all in the handling.'

'Why not?' he said to her, grinning.

She shrugged.

'We're free agents, aren't we?'

'Yes,' said Imelda, 'we're certainly that.'

So it was wordlessly agreed. From textiles to kitchens, from dining interiors to children's furniture, they could make believe they were starting all over again.

Katie *is* starting over. Her boyfriend left her when he found out she became pregnant by retrieving the just-used condom from the bin and inseminating herself with the help of a Johnson & Johnson's cotton bud. She had never expected it to work but now she's eight months gone and desperate for a late-night plate of Ikea's Swedish meatballs.

What she couldn't tell Oli is that it wasn't just some crazy impulse. The truth is, she'd been dreaming of sperm for months. She saw their urgent heads and tails in the quivering seeds of the tomatoes she sliced in the KFC kitchen. She saw them every evening in the paisley scarf of the businesswoman at her bus stop. She saw them in the Arsenal strikers who propelled themselves towards the goal as Oli shouted at the telly. She saw them in the spray of fireworks that lit up the night sky over the common on New Year's Eve. She'd even pointed heavenwards to the white, wriggling tails of light and whispered in Oli's ear over the crackle of static. 'Remind you of anything?'

'Yeah,' said Oli. 'Stickleback.'

Later Simone would say, 'What did I tell you, K? He's pond life.' Simone has been Katie's best friend since primary school. Katie persuaded her to come tonight to help her decide on a cot and changing table. Then they'll hit the food hall. Simone is not eating for two. Simone will be eating for Simone, and then some, as usual. It's only four days to Valentine's and there isn't a man in sight. She never told Katie she fancied Oli. It went without saying. She always fancies Katie's boyfriends. It is a dogged form of loyalty. Simone admires Katie. Simone lives through Katie. And, at times, though she doesn't know it, Simone envies Katie. She envies her her *fullness* – now more than ever of course. Because Simone never feels full in any sense of the word.

'Ten minutes to meatballs,' she announces.

Tonight, she too is suffering Katie's abandonment by Oli. Tonight she also rubs her lower back as the night wears on in the Ikea car park. And when the two lesbians in the queue ahead mistake her for being pregnant as well, she, along with Katie, accepts the offer of a fold-up chair and settles into it with the ancient gravitas of a matriarch-to-be.

In a state of chaos, change is not controlled by a source outside the system. On the contrary, it is determined by the myriad interactions of the elements within the system. The whole is greater than the sum of its parts.

Under the floodlights of the store, the ceremonial log is lowered into place, Swedish style. John Monaghan picks up the axe and begins to chop, wishing not only that he could loosen his belt, but also that he could simply snip a ribbon like any other retail manager. The effect, however, is not lost on those who wait. As the axe strikes its final blow, midnight arrives. The doors swing open and the crowd surges forward.

There is a race to Livingroom Interiors. Leather sofas, usually on sale for £325, are going for just £49 to the first 350 customers. Allan is among the sprinters. The finer points matter little to him. He stops only long enough to scribble the all-important code number before making a dash for Bedrooms. Good to be fit, he thinks.

He stops dead.

He knows the slender shoulders under the chunky cardigan. He knows the streaky blonde knot of hair. Julia.

Julia, his Julia, is standing with her back to him in Kitchens, opening and closing cupboard doors. She's standing next to a man who is looking at colour chip cards and investigating the undersides of kitchen units. Julia is with a man who doesn't mind shopping at Ikea.

Allan drops his code numbers and tries to flee. Only there's no room for manoeuvre. The crowd is dense and impatient behind him. 'I dare you to try, mate,' says a strapping Australian in a Man U shirt. Across the aisle in Livingrooms, people are diving on to sofas and staking their claims like squatters. Two couples are pulling on either end of his chosen settee in a consumer tug-of-war. Whatever made him think he could do this?

'Hello, Allan.'

Julia.

Julia.

'Fancy seeing you here,' she says.

'Likewise,' he says.

'Allan, this is Steve. Steve, Allan.'

Steve works out.

'Enjoying the bachelor pad?' Julia says.

'You bet.'

She pulls her cardi tight across her chest. Steve tactfully turns his attention to the spotlight-track set overhead. Allan grinds his teeth.

He wants to pull Julia into a quiet corner of the Tidaholm oak kitchen. He wants to say, What are you thinking? Will *Steve* stroke your back so you can sleep? Will *Steve* show you the secret lanes of Sussex by bike? Will *Steve* remember that, if you cry too much, your blepharitis flares up?

Shoppers shoulder past. 'It's crazy in here,' she says, smiling weakly.

'Crazy,' he agrees. So crazy, in fact, he can't stop himself. 'So, Steve,' he says, pulling his shoulders back, 'always take your dates to Ikea?'

'Come on,' says Julia, grabbing Steve's bicep. 'We're leaving.'

Steve doesn't blink. 'We're not dating.'

And Allan feels the sweet flood of relief.

'We're moving in together.'

It's one of those random puns of timing. As Allan mines his brain for an adequate response, someone in the amassing crowd pushes hard from behind. Allan lurches forward, pushing Steve in turn, who is sent stumbling backwards into Julia's dream kitchen range. As Steve gets to his feet, his large builder's hand is already curling into a raw-knuckled fist, and it is the sudden impact of said fist on Allan's right eye that marks the flagship store's point of no return.

Bob sees the whole thing from Children's Furniture, where Imelda is lingering by the bunk beds. Bob, ex-logistics manager, is a good man in an emergency. As the crowd turns ugly, he finds cover for Imelda under a starry bed-tent, then works his way back downstairs. By the time he reaches the front doors, he's seen it all: female shoppers being pushed out of the way by male shoppers; security guards dazed by the growing stampede; a man with a mallet. 'You have to close the doors,' he breathes to the doormen. 'It's complete and utter chaos up there.'

'We've only just opened,' says one.

'We don't have the authority,' says the other.

'Either you close the doors or I do,' says Bob.

Katie is the last person in the queue to be admitted before the doors are shut and locked. Simone is stranded outside, pressing her face to the glass, pudgy and wild eyed. 'You have to let my friend in,' Katie says to Bob. 'We came together.'

'Give it half an hour, love. When the place clears a bit, they'll open the doors again.'

'But we'll never find each other by then,' she pants. 'I got no charge left in my phone.'

'I can let you back outside to wait with her, but I can't let anyone else in. They're wall to wall upstairs.'

The need for Swedish meatballs is pushing on Katie's brain. She can already taste the beef gravy and cream. She's longing for the lingonberry preserve. But Simone's nose is white, piggy and pleading against the glass.

Katie turns to Bob. 'I'm eight months gone,' she sobs. 'Do you want me to drop here and now with the stress?'

Bob casts his eyes downward and sighs. He signals to the doorman. 'Okay. Just her, there.'

A door is unlocked and Simone pushes through.

She's not the only one.

Nick has been working his way up the row, helplessly drawn to the burgeoning belly that is Katie. He's come too close to be separated now. Is it her luminous skin? The lush weight of her hair? The bounty of her breasts? Or her general attitude of ripeness? It is impossible to rationalize, even for Nick, a young man prone to living in his head. Suddenly, instinct has caught him by the jugular, and he's damned if he's going to lose her now. He jumps the queue. He slides through the door, inches behind Simone.

Unfortunately, inspired by his lead, so do another four thousand.

Rachel and Aisling, dilly-dallying in Home Accessories, cast one look back over their shoulders, drop their fold-up chairs and make a dash for higher ground. 'It's a bloody rat-trap in here!' shouts Aisling on the run.

'We've got this far, haven't we?' shouts Rachel. 'And we're not leaving without that bed!'

In spite of her eight-month girth, Katie overtakes the couple, panicking at the thought of a run on meatballs. She is followed – blindly, recklessly – by Nick, who is followed in turn by Simone. Simone is slow to catch up, but quick to spot the new object of her affections. Already she fancies Nick, because she has divined, in the heat of his pursuit, that here is Katie's boyfriend-to-be.

All five – Simone, Nick, Rachel, Aisling and Katie – are only moments ahead of the moving wall of Ikea devotees.

Rachel, ever the midwife, gets hold of Nick's elbow as he overtakes her. 'Is she your partner?' she says sternly, nodding ahead to Katie.

'Yes,' he declares, his own lie taking him by surprise. 'Yes, she is.'

'Well, get her home pronto, young man. This is no place.'

'No . . . Of course. I will.'

'Come on, Rache!' yells Aisling.

But Rachel's phone is vibrating in her pocket. She flips it open, plugs her ear with a finger and breaks into a run again. 'Right *now*?' she shouts. She looks at Aisling, wide-eyed.

'Your overdue lady,' pants Aisling.

'My overdue lady,' pants Rachel.

'I'm coming with you.'

'No, I'm going back for the shuttle. You take the car.' She stops, takes hold of Aisling's hand and presses it in hers. 'The bed. You're getting us the bed if it's the last thing you do.' Then Rachel turns and walks like a virgin sacrifice into the oncoming crowd.

Nick catches up with Katie at the door of the Food Hall. 'Listen to me. You don't know me, but you shouldn't be here. It's not safe. I'm getting you out of here, okay?' and in that singular moment, Oli, her ex-sperm donor, is history.

'But my meatballs,' Katie breathes. 'I *need* meatballs.'

'We so do,' breathes Simone.

Suddenly, fleetingly, Nick understands what it is to be that thing he has never been: a man of action. He jumps the foodhall queue and commandeers a takeaway for two.

'And the cot!' cries Katie, her mouth poised to receive the first meatball from her plastic fork. 'What will I do without a cot?'

They storm Children's Furniture, where Imelda, still sheltering beneath her bed-tent, peeks out and smiles. 'How far along are you, love?'

'Eight months,' says Katie, licking jelly off her thumb.

Nick grabs an Ikea pad and pencil. He scribbles down the warehouse location numbers, and onwards the three run, like contestants in some terrible reality-TV game, 'Shop or Drop'.

It is in the Self-Service Warehouse that Katie suddenly fears she will.

'Oh my God!' she cries.

'Oh my God!' agrees Simone.

Katie pants, planting her hands on her knees. 'I need the toilet.'

'The toilet,' says Simone.

'The meatballs,' explains Katie.

'The meatballs,' nods Simone.

Katie whispers something in Simone's ear.

'And she's wet herself,' Simone announces to Nick.

'Simone!'

'She's having the baby,' says Nick. His gut churns.

'I am *not* having the baby!' barks Katie.

'We've another month to go,' Simone informs him, smugly.

Shoppers are pouring into the warehouse, hundreds by the minute. Merchandise is flying from the shelves. Arguments are spreading from aisle to aisle, with the relentless rhythm of a Mexican wave. Over the public-announcement system, Manager John Monaghan is begging his customers to remain calm.

In the opposite aisle, through the crowd, Nick spots the head of the friend of the woman who told him to get Katie home. She's a woman too, thinks Nick. Women are hard-wired with the facts.

Aisling is on the verge of lowering the last Noresund lacquered-steel bed frame on to her flatbed trolley when Nick appears, as white-faced and stricken as a father-to-be.

'Do you mind if I borrow that trolley?' he asks. 'We seem to have an emergency situation on our hands . . .'

She looks at Nick. She looks at the flatpack. She looks at Nick again.

'Better luck next time, sweetheart,' says a burly shopper as he walks away with her bed frame.

By the time she and Nick make it back through the crowd, Katie is in the seismic grip of her second contraction. She sits down on the edge of the trolley, groaning. 'Three minutes apart,' says Nick, checking his watch.

Aisling's lips twitch.

'I want the toilet!' Katie sobs.

'She wants the toilet!' sobs Simone. 'Can you walk, K?'

Aisling pulls out her phone and dials 999. 'An ambulance, please.'

It's five long minutes and a contraction later before she is connected. 'ETA: ninety minutes, if you're lucky,' says the controller. 'The North Circular's blocked in your direction. And we've got other Ikea calls. A stabbing. Someone else with chest pains. Crush injuries. We'll get to you as soon as we can.'

'Two minutes,' reports Nick as Katie doubles up again. 'Those last two were only two minutes apart.'

Katie moans.

Simone moans more.

Five miles away, Rachel is measuring a dilated cervix. 'Can you see the crown, Ash?' she mutters into her headset.

'How do I bloody know if you can see the crown?'

'*Look.*'

Aisling lowers the phone. Her eyes squeeze shut. 'Nick, listen to me. You are going to clear this aisle immediately. Simone, you are going to look at Katie and you are going to tell me if you can see the head.'

'See the head where?'

'*There.* Where do you think?'

Simone swallows and gets down on the floor. She spreads Katie's legs, peeks under her pink thong, and surfaces at last. 'No head but . . . there's a mega big bulge that just isn't natural if you ask me.'

Katie starts to howl.

'That *is* the head, silly girl!' Aisling turns away from the mother-to-be and mumbles into the phone. 'Does that mean it's going to be premature?'

'No, she's okay. She's past the twenty-eighth week.'

'But it's too quick for the first, isn't it? Something's wrong.'

'Nobody's a textbook, Ash. She's young, healthy. Chances are she's perfectly fine.'

'I need the toiiii-let!' screams Katie.

'If she wants to push,' instructs Rachel, 'get her to pant.'

'She wants the toilet.'

'Do *not* let her go to the toilet. Get her on to one of their beds and ring me again. She's about to have an Ikea home birth.'

At the far edge of any chaotic system – new order.

It takes only a moment for Aisling to remember who she is: a senior staff nurse who has frequently seen off Death. She summons all her brusque authority and hijacks the nearby service lift. Nick wheels Katie inside. Simone squeezes in before the doors rattle shut.

They are returned to the main display area where the crowd has, thankfully, thinned. The front line in the consumer battle has shifted to the warehouse downstairs. Aisling issues shopping lists to Nick and Simone. Then she surveys Bedrooms.

Noresund bed frame: £129. Storfors sprung mattress: £140.

How lucky, she thinks, that they encourage you to try out their furniture in store.

When Simone and Nick return with the plunder, she pulls off the Alvine Blommig bedspread (£35) and smoothes out the Sannie shower curtain (£9, machine washable). She helps Katie to sit at the edge of the bed with her hips hanging off and her knees apart.

She covers her with a bath towel (Saxan, £4.90). She positions the work lamp (Morker, £3).

'Now what?' she says to the phone wedged in her neck.

Katie is crying. Nick is chewing his knuckles.

'Get the father to talk to her and to keep talking to her. Tell him to keep her head cool with a damp tea towel or something. Where's her friend?'

'She's just coming now, with water from the food hall. Nick, get over here. Talk to Katie.'

'And no doctor has responded to the public announcement?'

'Rache, you can't even *hear* the public announcements.'

'Okay, you're ready.'

'Don't say that.'

'They practically deliver themselves, remember?'

'I need drugs!' sobs Katie. 'My birth plan says yes to every drug!'

'*And* we wanted a water birth!' wails Simone as she enters the scene, sloshing.

'Oh my God!' Aisling splutters. 'The head's really coming now.'

'See? What did I tell you? Get in there, Ash. Support it as soon as you can.'

'I'm going to die!' howls Katie. 'Simone, I never guessed I was going to die tonight!'

'Nick,' says Aisling, looking up, '*what* did I tell you to do?'

Nick climbs on to the bed, edging close. 'Katie?'

'Where's the . . . the' – she gulps breath – 'doctor?!'

'She's a nurse. This woman is a nurse.'

'Yeah,' says Simone from the other side of Katie's legs. 'She works with, like, dying people.'

Katie screams.

'Oh my God,' says Aisling.

'What? What's wrong?' says Rachel in her ear.

'The head. It's going crooked, towards her . . . her thigh.'

'Not a problem. Where's the cord?'

'I don't know – I can't see it. Simone, hold this bloody phone to my ear while I –'

Katie's eyes are swelling shut with her tears. 'I'm going to die!'

Nick grabs her hand. 'Katie? Katie, listen to me. Hold my hand, right? As hard as you like. No, don't look down there. Over here. I want you to look over here. At me. Can you do that for me?'

She's up on her elbows, her chin wedged tight against her windpipe.

He stacks pillows high to support her back. 'Okay. Here's the deal. You're going to look at me, Katie, and I'm going to look right back at you. The whole time. Got it?'

'I want to go home!'

'What colour are my eyes?'

She blinks back her tears, sniffs and focuses slowly. 'They're bloodshot.'

'Good girl. My eyes are bloodshot, and yours, yours are blue. Blue like . . . like those little spring flowers.'

'Which ones?'

'Forget-me-nots. Yeah? And whatever is going on down there, I'm right here. You're looking at me, I'm not going anywhere and you're not dying. Got it?'

Quietly, so only he can hear. 'Got it.'

Across town, Rachel adjusts her Bluetooth. 'And the cord's definitely not around the neck, Ash?'

'No, it's – oh my God, there's a shoulder . . .'

'Keep supporting the head, Ash. But don't pull.'

'And another . . .'

'Okay, the rest of the body's going to come quickly now.'

'And it's been so dull up to now.'

'Hold on 'cos they're slippery.'

'You're telling me? Christ, it's coming . . .'

'Hips?'

'For sure.'

'Bum.'

'Oh my God . . .'

'What's wrong?'

'I can't believe I'm doing this. Give me the death rattle any day. Oh my God, oh my God . . .'

'You've got it?'

'I've . . . Jesus.'

'Ash, you there?'

'I've –'

'What's going on?'

'I've –'

'Talk to me, Ash.'

'– got it.'

'You star!'

'How does it look?'

'Um. Not pretty.'

'Beneath the blood and that waxy stuff, it will be slightly bluish. That's okay.'

'Do I slap it?'

'No one does that any more.'

'Child abuse?'

'Unnecessary. Wrap it in a towel, then get it by its ankles.'

'Hey, I'm getting good at this.'

'Raise it so that its hips are slightly higher than its head.'

'Okay . . .'

'Which will allow its nose and mouth to drain, so it should' – a cry breaks through Ikea Bedrooms – 'cry almost immediately. Well done, Ash. You're brilliant. How's the mother?'

'Oh my God . . .' Aisling shakes herself and recalls the view beyond the birth canal. 'Katie, how are you?'

Katie is purple, dazed and hot. She hasn't yet released Nick's fingers from the deadlock of her grip. 'Is it okay?'

'Everything is fine.'

'A boy or a girl?'

Aisling blinks. She lifts a corner of the towel. 'A boy.' She studies him for a moment, then smiles at the couple. 'And, if I'm any judge, I'd say he looks like his daddy . . .'

Rachel is talking in her ear. 'So everyone's okay?'

'Unbelievably, yes.'

'One last question, Ash, then I'm needed again here.' She lowers her voice to a whisper. 'What about the *bed*?'

Aisling surveys the aftermath with a cool eye. She decides she'd recommend the Sannie shower curtain to anyone. 'Sorted,' she says.

Nick records the time of birth with his Ikea pad and pencil. Katie looks down, beholding the baby on her tummy. Simone slumps, exhausted, in a Gunghult rocking chair.

From beneath her bed-tent in Children's Furniture, Imelda hears the cry of a newborn and, emboldened by old instinct, follows the sound, half asleep, to the small group hovering around the dream bed. It's one-fifteen. The store was forcibly shut for business a half-hour ago. The paramedics are on their way to cut the cord. Ikea Security, who caught the last ten minutes of the drama on an in-store security camera, have drawn protectively close. Store manager, John Monaghan – who was in early discussions with Bob about a management vacancy – has been alerted. He and Bob are taking the stairs two at a time, eager to check on mother, child and Imelda.

Nick will prove an excellent father, unusually able to cope with little sleep. Katie will be pregnant again within eighteen months, as both she and Nick discover their mutual passion for procreation. They will name their firstborn Ingvar, after Ikea's founder.

Ingvar will not be quite like other children. Born into the chaotic night of 10 February 2005, he will labour under a certain confusion. He will struggle to learn how to tie his shoes. His limited eye-hand-and-foot coordination will make tree-climbing difficult and swimming lessons near fatal. He will be slow to pick up the natural rhythm and tones of his mother tongue, so many of his teachers will initially think Swedish his first language.

Yet he will try hard to tell his mother about the fluid dynamics he sees in the drip of the bathroom tap. He will look overhead to the movements of migrating birds and predict the subtlest of gestures within the flock. On weekends, he will show his father the bifurcating beauty of ancient branch and root systems in Lea Valley Park. At the age of ten, he will impress his music teacher with an uncanny intuition for the sacred music of Bach.

Ingvar, in short, will have a genius for complexity.

Years later, at Aylward Comprehensive, he will draw for Allan, his geography teacher, their receding native woodland in bright, dizzying fractals. He will be the first of Allan's pupils to feel, with him, the secret tug of the earth's buzzing core. At night, he will dream dreams he won't remember of the strange attractors of its magnetic fields. And, on Sundays, as he pushes his mother's Ikea flatbed trolley through the Edmonton store where he first drew breath, he will hear it, in spite of the press of shoppers; in spite of the 300,000-square-foot of box-store. He will hear it: the mute cadences of the earth's secret flux. Of the world unfolding, minutely.

Where there is milk, where there is honey

Come. Simon says come.

I nearly said it. Then she would have had to come. If I said it once, if I said it again. But something in her face said it could not be said. It told me she would have turned me away.

I wanted us to be there, we two, where the lights go on and on. Where there is milk, where there is honey.

That day time was crashing so fast it was hard to stop my feet; hard to stand still in the toppling tide of up-ramps and down-ramps. But I did. I stopped short, gripping the edge of her desk. She thought it was like any other time when I stopped in front of Nursie Station B. I'd always stop and stare. I'd just have to say it once and *say* it again.

'Simon says, have a p-p-pleasant day, Pinkie.' That's what I called her.

'Thank you, Simon.'

'Simon *s-s-says*.'

'Well, I'll certainly try, Simon.'

I stood staring. A food cart bumped along between us. Cabbage and broccoli steam puffed out like a fart you could see. 'I know where there's more food.'

'Mmm?' She was looking at papers on her desk.

'In the Superstore.'

'Very good, Simon. Well said.'

'I say a lot m-m-more than that.'

'I'm sure you do.'

'In my head, I say it smooth. Simon s-says it once. Then Simon *says* it again and I c-c-can do it.'

'Very good.'

She wanted me to go away. Her pretty head was bent so she didn't have to see me. I was drooling slightly on her desk. My hair had not been combed. My face was stubble black. I knew I didn't smell right. Pinkie was fearful. Her hair was all smooth and stuck together, but it was only the bright lacquer of her hair spray that kept her fear under control.

'What are you doing, Simon?' She was staring at my zipper. Then I saw my hand – gripping the anchor of myself through the hole in the lining of my pocket. Pinkie anchored me whenever I saw her. She held me fast to the world.

'Go back to your room now, Simon.'

I told my carpet slippers to move, but only the once. So they stayed and I stayed looking. I said, 'Pinkie, c-c-come.' My voice was a thin wind whistling in my head.

She looked up. 'Hmmm?'

'Crumb, I said. Bread crumbs: twelve cents per quarter pound.'

'Is that right?'

'Y-yes. Good for fish b-b-batter. Grandad fished cod and blue-fish. S-s-sometimes lobster. He'd set them scuttling on the kitchen floor till the p-p-pot was ready. Then he'd b-beat them down with the wooden spoon till the l-l-lid was on.'

Another nursie was at the desk now. She had no eyebrows. Only greasy brown lines she drew on each day. Pinkie was talking to her through barely moving lips.

Carpet slippers across the floor. Simon *says*. Shuffle shuffle.

There was a time when I could have said come. Said it once, said it twice. But time rolled in a wave over my head and my thoughts got tangled in the weed, like Grandad's traps after a storm-churned day. It was Arts & Crafts. It was Pinkie's turn to sit in the chair behind Teacher and keep an eye, but her chair was empty still.

Only at juice-and-Wagon-Wheels time did she run in, nearly

tripping over Tom's false leg. I could tell she wasn't well. Her coat was dark with the soak of the rain, and her hair lay in wet, sticky streaks across her forehead. She took off her coat. Her blouse had escaped the tuck of her pinafore. Her pinstripes were crooked, and there were arcs of sweat under her arms. I watched her dab her nursie shoes and tights with a Kleenex, but she was making the mud worse.

We were making Popsicle-stick lighthouses that day. Teacher was going from table to table, counting in her head everyone's share of sticks so that her old furred lips moved silently with the numbers but not as silently as she thought. By now Pinkie was trying to fix herself in a little mirror she had taken from her purse. She wiped away dribbles of black that ran from her eyes. She tried to smooth down her hair with a pat here and a pat there. But she wouldn't come right.

It didn't help when she saw Tom scratching his false leg. Or Emma, the half-dressed schoolteacher, counting up to thirty-three with her sticks. I just sat in my fold-up chair, sipping from my straw and crying. Crying for the fear of my nursie-girl and her hair that was flying away. I wanted to say, poor, poor girl in your pink-striped pinafore, come with me. Come to the Superstore.

I wanted to tell her about the shiny gold cans of hair spray, row after row. About the mirrors on the walls behind Fruits & Vegetables where she might forever put herself together. Then there was that music, those melodies so soft in the back of your ear. Better than a pill on your tongue. They'd make her forget about Tom and his itchy plastic leg.

'There's no need,' she was saying to Emma, who was on number 26. 'No need at all.'

She looked at me looking at her and crying. There was a wrinkle in Pinkie's smooth forehead. She knew I knew. She knew that I knew that she was this close to not knowing the difference between her and us. More than ever I wanted to say, it's not too late . . . Not too late to come to the Superstore with me. There's MORE in the Superstore. Not just aisles and aisles but smiles and smiles.

'Why are you crying, Simon?' Her pink pinstripes widened into bars in front of me. You would never know that anything had ever been crooked. 'What do you want?'

'MORE,' I said sniffling.

'Juice?'

'No,' I sobbed.

'A Wagon Wheel? You want one now?'

'No!'

'I'll bring you more sticks. You can have extra sticks. Your lighthouse will be the tallest.'

She laid a small pile at my side. I was still crying snotty tears. As she showed me how to turn a red Christmas tree ball into the beacon for the lighthouse, I raised my hand and touched her hair.

'Time to make your beacon, Simon.' Her voice was firm. Her hair was under control once more. She would never now be mine.

'A store is m-m-more,' was all I could say.

'Whatever you like then. Make whatever you like.'

I was at sea in my grandfather's Cape Islander and my anchor was gone.

And that's why I could only say crumb though I wanted her to come as I stared as she sat behind Nursie Station B. That's why I had to go alone in the end.

I left Pinkie talking to the nursie under the greasy arches as I went all the way to the front door. All the way to on my way. I told myself it would be like the other times. I had only to walk past the porter with the hat that falls over his eyes, and through the revolving door. Only, suddenly, I was looking at the porter and he at me. They had given him a new hat and it sat square on his head so I was looking into his eyes for the first time. They were sharp, like the knives they use in the kitchen to dig the black eyes from potatoes. I tried hard to keep my eyes from going big and black in the white of my potato face.

'Going somewhere, Simon?'

'To the S-S –'

'To the Superstore again, eh? What for? Plenty to be had right here, right? Everything you need.'

'Everything I need,' I repeated, but I couldn't stop staring at the revolving door. People were going round and round, women turning into men turning into children turning into old people. Suddenly I remembered a merry-go-round from a place I didn't know any more. Jump on, they had said. Come on, jump! But I was too afraid.

'You head back to your room now, Simon. Lunch in a few hours.'

Shuffle shuffle.

In my room, I open my window. I do not hear the barks of gulls. I do not smell the ocean. When I ask where the ocean is, they smile and tell me, exactly where I left it. There is a patch of a courtyard with a dying maple tree in the centre. Its branches reach in a tangle up to my window. At the bottom, concrete slabs surround its trunk. It is time to jump ship.

My leg is through the window. More bone than leg. I put one carpet slipper on to the difficult branch. Brave. Be brave, Simon. The concrete slabs look unmissable. Simon *says* be brave. I put all my weight on the branch. It groans like my old grandad when he died last year of pneumonia. He left me the *Reverence*, his nets and traps, his night-fishing lanterns, and his Queen of Heaven rosary that always hung above the radio. He left it to me because there was no one else.

My slippers fly from my feet. I don't look down. That's the trick, everyone says. I'm looking straight ahead, over the red rooftops where all the families live; homes so square I can almost forget the wild of these unwieldy branches and my heart reeling. And there, beyond the rooftops and the barbed-wire of the TV antennae, I can see it. The big neon letters: SUPERSTORE. Not far now.

I go down and down until my toes hit ground and wriggle against the cold of it. I take my slippers from the roots of the tree. The day is damp. Someone has forgotten to turn off the street lights. They burn yellow in the dirty grey of morning. No need. I know where I'm going. Just one block, two, to go.

Those are faces in the fog of that window. Children's faces drizzling tears down the window panes. I want to say, come to the Superstore with me, open twenty-four hours a day. It's never grey in the Superstore. But they are staring at my slippers that go flap against the soles of my feet, and a woman comes suddenly to the window.

In the parking lot, I pass yellow line after yellow line. Yellow lines that stay yellow even in the rain, even after the rain, even after you and me. I run so fast that one slipper flies into a puddle, black and purple and green with the car grease that floats on top. No matter now that I'm here. I might even get a new one at the Superstore. Anything is possible now.

The doors slide away with my footfall. Like Open Sesame.

Sesame seed buns: aisle 4. I know it.

And there, right there, are the bright candy-red gum machines. Double-trouble. Jawbreakers. Sweethearts. Good & Plenty. I pull out a quarter and slip it in the slot. I catch the two small squares of chewy pink in both hands and unwrap them greedily. I slap my thigh at the wisecracks of Balooka Jo, then offer the comic to a child who's telling me she can't talk to strangers. Balooka Jo's no stranger, I say. I'm blowing a bubble, bigger than my face, and everything goes rosy: the child, the shopping carts, the horse that goes giddy-up for a dollar, even my slipperless foot.

And I'm walking. I walk towards myself who is walking towards me in a black-and-white TV. I've never been on TV before. I'm waving. I'm blowing another bubble. This one's for you, Pinkie, I announce live, on air.

Everything is as it should be. I smile at a pretty blonde cashier and she smiles back. Not just aisles and aisles but smiles and smiles. I hum along with a tune that drips from the ceiling. Dee da dee, da dee da dum . . . And the light that goes on and on is breaking over every tin of soup, sardines and fruit cocktail, like sun on a silver wave.

Frozen Foods now. Butterscotch ripples golden through containers of ice cream. Over at the Deli, squares of processed cheese slices make orange-and-white checkerboards in the display case. I wander into Cereals. 'Looks like rain today, sir.'

It's the stockboy. At first, I don't trust myself to speak, but there's no need to fear in the Superstore. His eyes, bright as new nickels, say as much.

'Yes,' I say, say it smooth. 'But it's always n-nice in the Superstore.' I'm staring at his price gun. 2.69 2.69 2.69 2.69 2.69 2.69 2.69 2.69 2.69 2.69 2.69 2.69 2.69 2.69 2.69 2.69 2.69 2.69 2.69 2.69 2.69 2.69 I've never seen one in motion. 1.88 1.88 1.88 1.88 1.88 1.88 1.88 1.88 1.88 1.88 My heart can't resist its rhythm. 1.88 runs swift in my blood.

'Are you all right?'

I make myself walk away, numbers leaping in my veins.

Around the corner, the candies invite. Hundreds of coins of red and peppermint green spill over the open bin. There are slabs of white almond-bark too and dreamy dark Chocolate Temptations, just 48 cents per half-pound. My mouth waters. It's only a reach away. No one is looking.

Simon says, I dare you. Just a taste. My hand reaches . . . it's nearly there in the chocolate dream. A spinster of a woman scooping up jelly babies turns and stares at me. My hand closes into a fist and I shove it back into my pocket.

Two rows over, the Superstore hostess in her fresh white smock is offering cheese and crackers to the morning shoppers.

I take a broken cracker from the plate she holds out to me. Her teeth are so white. I know those teeth. Then it comes to me. She's the girl on the Pepsident Toothpaste box. And here she is, offering me cheese on a toothpick. Wouldn't Grandad slap his leg at the thought.

I pass Fresh Produce, rich pickings laid out on grass greener than I've ever known. It is always summer in the Superstore. There are peaches, rounds of gold and rose with hairs that catch the fluorescent light. There are baby potatoes so clean you'd never know they were lifted from the earth by human hands. This is Paradise. This fruit, these vegetables, shall not wither.

There's a long, loud whirring coming from behind me. I turn. The butcher is at the Meat Counter, grinding mounds of beef into soft twists of red. Pork shanks are today's Special Saver. Compare with the rest, then come back to the best.

I never want to leave. Not ever no way.

I did not mean to go down aisle 8. I was heading for aisle 7: Cleaning Products. But the thought of Lysol and linoleum caught in my nostrils and made me turn away. Now I'm in Aisle 8 and there they are. One slim gold can after another. New Formula 17. Staying power so your hair won't have straying power. Pinkie's brand. I'm sure of it.

It's going to rain today. Maybe she hasn't remembered her plastic rain hat. Or her umbrella. Oh for the thought of her hair coming undone, and Pinkie with it. Everyone is so easily dishevelled in this world.

I start to sweat at the thought of it. Antiperspirants, aisle 6. How can she feel better than us if I'm not there to help her feel like herself? Forgive me, my nursie-girl.

I stare at the golden cans of Formula 17. Simon says, take it. Simon *says*.

I'm running fast but it seems as though everything is running past me faster still; that I'm not running at all. There goes the butcher, the shampoos, the cleansers, the Pepsident Lady, the spinster with her jelly babies, the girl at the checkout. I'm a blur on the overhead TV . . . But will the doors open? I hear the almighty crash of a broken sea of bottles as the bottle bank is emptied. A Superstore boy passes me, wrestling a long scorpion's tail of shopping carts. Will it ever end? Please let me leave the Superstore! I cannot stay.

The butcher is after me and yelling things. I'm in the parking lot. My last slipper flies below a white Chevrolet. The dog inside starts to bark and froth. There's green bottle glass on the pavement, green glass in my feet . . . Then the butcher's on me, his meaty shanks pinning my legs.

The pretty cashier is somewhere behind us. 'Don't hurt him, Jim. He's one of them from the Villa.'

They bring me back. Pinkie is at Nursie Station B. She smiles at them like she is meaning, couldn't be helped, and they all shrug their shoulders and smile some more. Pinkie peeks over the desk and sees the smear of blood from my feet on the yellow linoleum. She says to go with the other nurse. She will get the glass out of my feet and bandage them.

But I stay and stare at her as always. I have to be sure.

'Simon?' says the other nurse.

Pinkie is looking at me like she doesn't know me. She is smiling easily. Everything is clear. 'Well, what does Simon have to say for himself today?'

I am looking at her hair, smooth and shining with spray-on light. She is the Queen of Heaven. She is the light of the day. My anchor strains again below my zipper. It grounds me to the world.

'Simon? I asked you something, now, didn't I?'

I unzip my trousers. I give thanks.

The Will Writer

No, he replies, no, he plans ahead; he's someone who likes to be prepared. So he had no trouble finding the house. He always checks his route carefully using one of the internet street-locators.

'How clever,' she says, taking his overcoat.

He smiles, feeling the heat of a blush climb up his neck and over his collar as Mrs Richardson ushers him into the sitting room. 'There are those who wouldn't be having it,' he adds, 'but I must say, I rather enjoy life on the road. You see, as soon as I'm out of the car park at Head Office, I'm essentially my own boss.'

'I'm sure.'

He takes a seat on an ample leather sofa. 'And there's the peace and quiet of a car. Your own home away from home, as the saying goes. *Not* that I'm not glad to have my wife and son to return to every evening.'

'Of course.' She's at the window, drawing a heavy set of drapes. 'What age is your son?'

'He's just turned seven.' He gives her a tentative smile. 'I suppose you could call me a late starter . . .'

Mrs Richardson tuts politely and pulls a neat mahogany tea trolley into place.

'The good thing is, I'm home most nights in time to read him – Michael – his bedtime story. At the moment, we're working our way through the pile of *Just William* books I read myself when I was a boy.'

The Skills Facilitator at Head Office says that it's important to let the client see that you're perfectly ordinary with perfectly ordinary concerns. And the will writer assures himself: he *is* perfectly ordinary. He has never had aspirations to be otherwise.

Mrs Richardson apologizes that her husband has not arrived home yet. He says, not to worry, though he must remind her that nothing, of course, can progress without *both* their signatures, as they've indicated interest in a joint will package. 'I can't imagine what the delay is,' she says as she passes him a cup of Earl Grey and a Duchy Originals shortbread biscuit.

He smiles reassuringly, snaps open his company-standard briefcase and lifts out a royal blue YOUR WILL folder.

'Do you have another appointment today?' she asks. On the folder she can see her name, her husband's name, and the words 'Will Deluxe Service'. It makes her want to laugh. It makes her want to laugh at this man who's come peddling death's wares. His trousers are too short, and he's wearing light socks with black shoes and garters that clip on to the socks. She hasn't seen those things in years. 'I'd hate it if we kept you.'

'No, you're fine,' he replies, straightening the flaps of his tie against the spread of late middle age. 'I had one appointment in Sutton after you but Head Office phoned just before I pulled up your drive to say the young couple in question were obliged to reschedule.'

'I see.'

From somewhere in the house an antique clock wheezes and chimes the quarter hour.

'I guess that goes with the territory,' Mrs Richardson adds.

'Hmm?'

'People rescheduling . . . trying to postpone the inevitable.' She smiles, as if at a shared joke, and he decides he rather likes her smile. It is delicate, even nervous by habit, he would guess, yet, just now, oddly reckless.

He relaxes slightly. 'The stories I could tell.'

'*Really*,' she says, and her grey eyes widen with mischief.

'The male of the species, I have to admit, is the worst.' He swallows the last of his Highland shortbread. 'Cowards, almost without exception. If I've learned anything after eighteen years in the business, it's that.'

'How so?'

'I can't tell you the number of men who have opened the door to me, drunk at three in the afternoon – you see, it's usually the lady of the house who makes the appointment.'

'*No.*'

'Once, when there was no answer at the front of a particular property, I took the liberty of going around to the back, and I spotted the couple through the kitchen window – a couple in their sixties, mind you – crouching on the floor next to the breakfast bar. I'm afraid I heard the whole sorry argument through the cat flap!' He listens to his own voice as it gathers strength in the tasteful surrounds of Mrs Richardson's sitting room. Yes, he can be entertaining when he chooses to be; when he deems it appropriate.

'I'm sure my husband will be home any time now.'

He nods. 'Did I point out that our Probate Department's fees would be at least 40 per cent less than those charged by any of the major banks?'

'You did, thank you.'

'And that, if you sign up to the Will Deluxe Service, Mrs Richardson, we will store your house deeds absolutely free in a fireproof, high-security vault.'

'I'll have to ask Mr Richardson but I believe they've been with our bank for absolutely yonks.'

He brushes biscuit crumbs from his napkin into his now empty tea cup. 'Have you had a chance to read the testimonials I posted to you?'

'Yes,' she says grinning. She can't help herself. '"Mr H of Milton Keynes says thank you,"' she recites. '"He could never have managed the whole terrible business on his own . . . Mrs

Trollope" – always an unfortunate name to marry into – writes,
"I'm very grateful. You've relieved my family and I" – ''me''
would be correct, I believe – "of a very heavy burden." '

'Yes,' he nods, hardly listening. He wonders if he can bring
himself to ask if he might use the cloakroom. Somehow the
request seems awkward without the presence of Mr Richardson.
'Over seventy thousand satisfied clients,' he adds.

'No doubt, Mr . . . Mr . . . ?' She feels giddy. The truth is, she
doesn't give a damn what the man's name is.

He reaches into his breast pocket and offers her his card.

'Oh look!' Mrs Richardson bends like a girl and, delighted,
picks up a blue paper ticket that has fallen from his jacket. 'Your
dry-cleaner, if he's anything like ours, will simply *torture* you if
you turn up without it.'

'Actually, it's a raffle ticket,' he confesses, and he wonders why
he said anything; why he should have spoken of it at all.

'A raffle? How exciting. What might you win? I'm potty for
all of it. Raffles. The National Lottery. The gee-gees. Russian
roulette when a dinner party gets dull, as they mostly do, even
my own, no, especially my own, though no one else ever seems
keen – on spinning the cylinder, that is – after the cheese and
biscuits. You must be the same. You must like the occasional
flutter, am I right?' Why, she wonders, does she feel drunk?
Hasn't she been dry for six months now?

'No,' he says, pretending to chuckle. 'I'm afraid not.' In his
line of work, it is important to appear calm, stable, yet friendly.
'I was just passing. A stall, I think, at the local shopping centre
while I waited for my wife to emerge from Tesco's. It's for a car.
Or maybe an SUV – that's a "Sports Utility Vehicle" to you and
me. A charity raffle. Not that there's any hope. Not that there
ever really is in these things.' He tucks the ticket very carefully
into his wallet.

'No,' she agrees, moving across the room to switch on a floor
lamp. 'Not that there ever really is.'

The will writer watches her face age unexpectedly as it is caught, briefly, in the light. He glances at his watch.

'Another cup of tea perhaps?' she offers.

'No, thank you. I'm fine – though, please, don't let me stop you.'

Thankfully, he is rarely lost for words. They discuss London's Congestion Charge, the state of the NHS, her son Joshua's summer wedding, seasonal rainfall averages, the latest property boom, and the reduction of postal services to just one delivery a day. At last the will writer gets to his feet. 'If you'll forgive me, Mrs Richardson, I'll leave you in peace. But you have my card and the number for Head Office – that's Croydon – should you and Mr Richardson wish to make another appointment.' He snaps his briefcase shut. He thanks her for the tea and biscuits. Privately, he decides he can wait till the next motorway services for the loo.

'Has it been raining?' she asks – herself more than him – as she passes him his damp overcoat. He slides into one sleeve, then the next, awkwardly. He is a big man, she observes. Burly even. Why didn't she notice as he sat, taking up room on her sofa? She opens the door and peers out. 'Will the days *ever* start getting longer?' Suddenly she is eager to have him on his way, gone, lost to the encroaching dark of the late-November afternoon.

'When your number's up, it's up. It doesn't matter if you live in Middle England or in the middle of a bombardment in bloody, barking Basra.'

It's the Exeter chap sounding off again. Everyone's off the road. Grounded for a staff-training day. On the radio in the canteen, a well-modulated voice is saying that no one knows how many Iraqis have been killed. Iraq Bodycount says 17,000. An Iraqi political group, People's Kifah, reports 37,000. The *Lancet* claims that Operation Iraqi Freedom may have led to as many as 98,000 civilian deaths.

The will writer unpeels the sweating cellophane from the sandwich he's bought from the machine. In spite of himself, he wonders if this new chap, the one from the Exeter office, is right; if there is a day, an hour, a moment on the clock when you have to punch out.

He smiles to himself. He rarely thinks like this. Unlike the 'cowards' he laughed about with Mrs Richardson, he is not susceptible to bouts of existential panic. Indeed, in planning for the deaths of others – day in, day out, year in, year out – it is surprisingly easy to forget that he himself is not exempt; that he is not so very ordinary that Death won't take notice of him some ludicrous day. Perhaps this is why, when asked to complete a recent Investors in People questionnaire, the will writer ranked his job satisfaction as 'high'.

Nor will he waver on that point when, on his way home tonight, from Croydon to Surbiton, he is cut up twice during the forty-minute drive: once on the A232, just before Hackbridge, and again on the A240, after the Beggar's Hill roundabout. He will blare his horn, braking only just in time. He will hit the foglights and tailgate each offending driver. He will hold his ground, relentless in the rear-view, until he or she is forced from the lane.

As his ready-meal defrosts in the microwave, the will writer finds the brochure he picked up at the stall and staples the ticket to it, so it can't go astray again. Number 1009. He paid £15 for it. DATE OF DRAW: November 30th.

Less than a week to go.

The brochure is already well thumbed. 'The Hummer SUV instantly became the most functional off-road vehicle ever made available to the civilian market. So what makes it the real deal? In a world where SUVs have begun to look like their owners, complete with love handles and mushy seats, the H2 proves that there is still one out there that can drop and give you 20.'

And doesn't the will writer himself do his best to stay in shape? Twenty press-ups and eighty sit-ups as part of his ten-minute callisthenics routine at the foot of his bed each morning.

He leafs forward: 'The Hummer Driving Academy is the ultimate experience for any Hummer owner. The H1 and H2 were created to handle deep water, nasty inclines and harrowing vertical ledges. On the same course where the US army and Allied Forces have trained drivers, you'll face twisted, muddy terrain . . . Unfortunately, after the training is over, you will have to return to civilization.'

And Croydon *is* civilization, make no mistake, thinks the will writer. Surrey. The Home Counties. Head Office. After all those years at the Leeds branch. He considers the colour he will choose, given the chance. He's narrowed it down to two: Stealth Gray Metallic and Desert Sand Metallic.

The microwave bleeps. He shakes himself from the desert sand, lopes into his kitchenette and switches the cooking dial on to high power. 'With the addition of a transfer case shield and a heavy plastic fuel tank shield,' he reminds himself, 'such complete undercarriage protection ensures that, even if you're in a HUMMER, the best offence is still a good defence.' He knows the words, even as the delicate, reckless Mrs Richardson knew those customer testimonials.

He knows, too, that nine point seven inches of ground clearance allows this premiere urban-assault luxury vehicle to clear obstacles, both on- and off-road. He knows that it can ford an impressive twenty inches of water, pass through deep ditches and traverse large dirt mounds without suffering any front- or rear-end damage. He knows the H2 can tow up to 6,700 lbs in the toughest situations; that it can scale a 60 per cent slope and climb a sixteen-inch vertical wall. The H2 has to exude power and authority. It has to inspire driver confidence. In a word, it has to be overbuilt.

Like the will writer himself. Six foot three in his bare feet.

With a strong frame. Like his grandfather before him, a Yorkshire man.

He doesn't bother with a plate, making do instead with the plastic tray provided. What's more, he recalls, shovelling forkfuls of chilli into his mouth, the integrated DVD Navigation System can be adjusted to switch between audio prompts and displayed text messages to help guide drivers. The OnStar Advisor includes services such as directions almost anywhere, searches for hard-to-find tickets for most major shows and sporting events, plus help with vacation planning. He smiles, shaking his head – whatever next? Why, you can even send a bouquet of flowers to your wife from the comfort of your driver's seat.

Yasmeen. She'd be Yasmeen. Arabic for Jasmine. He'd send her fresh bunches of the stuff on every anniversary, because he's sentimental. She'd have come to London on one of those English-as-a-Second-Language courses. She'd be lodging in Surbiton and struggling to make herself understood at the post office on the High Street when he'd ask if he could help.

He has always liked the idea of Arabian mystery; of soft, dusky skin and shaking bracelets.

She'd photograph him on her mobile phone and, giggling, send pictures of him to her girlfriends at the language school. That's how it would all begin.

He counts two roadside shrines today, the plastic wrap of the assorted flora twinkling in the early-morning sunshine. He spots the first at the site of a large and ancient oak as he sits in traffic on the edge of Nonsuch Park. A sad display of stiff carnations and fading chrysanths. The other is more plentiful, a blur of colour at a steel guard rail by a pedestrian crossing. When do people do it? he wonders. You never see anyone out there, with their scissors and twine and petrol-station bouquets. These things turn up, literally overnight, he decides, like graffiti. Like something slightly shameful.

At the office, where he hot-desks with three colleagues, there's a message waiting for him. Mr and Mrs Richardson have requested another appointment. For today if possible. Ring back to confirm.

'Mrs Richardson . . . Certainly. No, I understand . . . And that suits Mr Richardson . . . ? Jolly good . . . No, not to worry. She'll keep dinner for me – I'm afraid she knows all too well that it goes with the job . . . Yes. Righty-ho. Six it is then.'

He walks past the thin, chest-high partition wall that divides the will writers from the Your Will call centre. The company slogan flutters on a royal-blue banner overhead, caught in the stale breeze from the heating duct. YOUR WILL – WHERE YOUR WILL IS OUR COMMAND. Kirsty waves to him absentmindedly as she chirrups into her mouthpiece the greetings she reads off her flickering monitor. He waves back, then enters the Richardson appointment on the whiteboard on the back wall. His colour is black. Only the Exeter chap, in red, has been anything like serious competition on the numbers front in recent months. But while he's great at lining up the appointments, relying very little on the cold-callers in the office, he's less impressive at getting the signed deal. And, in the end, only a signed deal is the real deal.

The will writer scans his day. Mrs Ogilvie's at ten-thirty, wanting, no doubt, to change her will yet again to pit niece against nephew or nephew against second cousin. 'Such fun I have!' she grins, lopsidedly since the stroke. Or she's merely looking for company. Isn't she on the phone to Your Will every other week? The will writer begrudges the time he'll lose to her. Although she'll have to pay for the extra home visit, it's hardly going to help him hit this month's target. But Kirsty tends to put the widows and widowers his way. He's more well spoken than the other will writers, she says, and the older, more respectable client values that.

Yasmeen, he thinks, will value it too. He'll be able to speak for her in an impatient world. She won't be lost to the sea of asylum-seekers he sees swelling every morning on Wellesley Road, outside the Home Office, before its doors even open for the day.

Twelve-thirty is an introductory visit to a Mr Carradine and a Mr Pembury in Brighton. 'Gay as the day is long,' Kirsty smirks as she gives him the address. Then it's back to his own turf, Surbiton, for a two-thirty appointment, also introductory, with the newlyweds who had to cancel yesterday. 'Apparently,' Sheena informs him – Sheena's at the desk next to Kirsty's – 'the husband's got a fatal bee allergy. His throat could swell and close within a matter of *minutes*, and, to top it all off, he's always forgetting his Epi-thingamajig whenever he plays golf. Now, no word of a lie, by the time Kirsty finished with the poor wee wifie, she was in tears on the other end and practically *begging* for another appointment.'

He should be finished with the newlyweds by four, which leaves him time to swing by Burger King on his way out of Surbiton, eat, complete the day's paperwork, and be on the road again by five to reach Mr and Mrs Richardson by six, even allowing for rush-hour traffic. In eighteen years, he's never once been late. It's true, he's been tediously early, but he's never been late. As the Skills Facilitator says, it's important to show the client you're in control. 'At a time like that – when they face the grim task of weighing up their lives' worth – you're making it clear you're in charge, come what may.' And that, the will writer tells himself, is precisely what he does. He takes charge.

Except he didn't expect them to be Muslims. Sheena didn't say anything about the newlyweds being Muslims. Since when do you find Muslims on the golf courses of Surrey? It threw him, frankly. He found himself worrying about making accidental eye contact with the wife. Weren't there rules about that sort of thing? He was determined not to offend, but it didn't help that the coffee she served was as black as Saudi oil. Had he done the wrong thing by asking if they might have any Nescafé to hand instead? Worse still, he forgot key parts of his introductory patter because the husband kept murmuring 'Inshallah' after everything he said. The will writer found himself blushing, even before they both bent down to help him gather up the payment-plan leaflets that had slid from his lap.

No matter. He checks his watch. He's right on time. The wide arc of Mr and Mrs Richardson's drive beckons. It returns him to himself. He slides a breath-freshener strip on to his tongue and checks his teeth in the mirror for any bits of lettuce left over from his Chicken Royale.

Mr Richardson opens the door. He's a well-built man with a firm handshake and a shrewd face. Nothing drunk or cowardly about him, the will writer decides.

'Tea?' Mrs Richardson offers as he steps once more into the decorous calm of the sitting room.

'Or something a bit stronger?' asks Mr Richardson, taking the situation in hand. 'It's gone six, after all.'

'Thank you,' says the will writer, finding his former place on the leather sofa. 'But, much as I'd like to, it's only right I keep a clear head when attending to your business.'

'You don't mind if I do?'

'Not at all.'

'Felicity, anything for you?'

She looks up, her eyes narrowing. 'No,' she says slowly, 'not for me.'

He smiles at the will writer and rolls his eyes, as if to say, 'Women. What can you do?'

Mrs Richardson doesn't join in on the joke. 'Where did I leave those lists, Jack?'

'Lists? What lists?'

'The lists I was showing you this morning.' A strand of pale yellow hair keeps falling across her face as she rummages in the magazine rack by the sofa. 'The lists where we started to write out *which* things we'd like to go to *whom*.'

'The Personal Effects & Gift List,' adds the will writer, trying to be helpful.

Mr Richardson pours himself a shot of Jameson whiskey. 'I don't see how that matters just now, Felicity. It's the will itself that's important. That's the purpose of this meeting. There *are* fates worse than death and, the way I see it, "dying intestate" is one of them. When I first heard the word, for Lord's sake, I thought it was a type of impotence!'

He can joke about death, the will writer observes, for Mr Richardson too is a man in control.

'Surely we can simply send this Gift list' – he looks to the will writer for confirmation – 'surely we can just send it in by post whenever you're finished with the thing, Lissie.'

She straightens. 'When *I'm* finished with the thing?'

He looks perplexed. 'Yes.'

'Why, Jack, is it my job? Why, Jack, is everything my job?'

He brings his shot glass down somewhat too suddenly on the cherrywood mantelpiece. 'Because, Felicity, it so happens *I'm* the one who's dying. Forgive me if this means I must occasionally bow out of some of our forward planning!' He forces a laugh for the will writer's benefit.

'But they're *your* things, Jack. How am I going to know what to do with your fishing rods, for goodness sake? Only Josh had any interest in fishing and you know very well he turned vegetarian when he met Sophie.'

Mr Richardson rolls his eyes, again for the will writer's entertainment. 'My only son, a vegetarian.'

'Then there's your antique atlas collection. I suppose I could hold on to that in case India or Daniel become interested as they get older, but –'

'But, let's be honest,' he says, folding his arms across his broad chest, 'it requires a lot of dusting.'

'That's not fair, Jack.'

'Neither is a high-grade brain tumour, Felicity, but you don't see me fussing, do you?'

'No. I just don't see you at all. You're hardly home these days. Even Mr . . . Mr . . . can vouch for that. Most dying men at least make an effort to do the hearth-and-home scene. It's only seemly after all, but you, you won't make it as far as our next wedding anniversary, and you still can't tear yourself away from you-know-who.'

He downs his whiskey. 'Ruby, isn't it?'

'What did you say?'

'Our Ruby Wedding Anniversary. Forty years in April.'

She lowers herself into a wingback chair and crosses one leg over the other. 'Not now, Jack,' she says, lowering her voice. 'Don't play the romantic now.' In the other room, her heirloom clock wheezes and chimes. She looks up, shaking herself free of the sudden weight of memory, and seems to brighten. 'On second thought, yes. I'll have that drink. Why not? I'll have whatever you're having.'

Mr Richardson's thread-veined face stiffens. 'Now you know you, Lis,' he says, emphasizing each word, 'you know you'll be fast asleep before *EastEnders* even starts, and tomorrow you'll wonder where the evening went!'

'No. Really, Jack.' She folds her hands in her lap. 'I'll have – what is it? – a whiskey too.' She turns to the will writer. 'Are you sure we can't offer you something?'

'No.' He smiles shyly. 'Thank you all the same.'

Mr Richardson ignores his wife. 'Right,' he says, clapping his hands, 'where do we start?'

The will writer blinks, then snaps open his briefcase. 'Well, first I'll need to make sure I have the names and addresses of all your beneficiaries, as well as those of your trustees.'

He looks up. Across the room, Mrs Richardson sits very upright in her wingback chair. The drinks coaster she has placed on the side table next to her is bare. Tears run down her face.

The will writer clears his throat. Mr Richardson turns to his wife, sighs and digs for his hankie. 'Come on, Lis. We don't want a scene, do we? We really could do without a scene, don't you think?'

'I'll have that drink, Jack.'

He turns to the will writer and lowers his voice. 'It's difficult, of course. Of course it is. She's still adjusting to the news.'

'Liar,' she murmurs.

'Lissie . . .'

'My drink, please, Jack. You offered me one not two minutes ago.'

His smile is brittle as he looks from wife to will writer and back again. 'Lis, you know very well that you –'

She stares at the carpet as she speaks. 'I won't sign anything without it. Do you hear me, Jack? Your fancy-woman will have to sue to get as much as a pair of monogrammed cuff links.'

'How many times do I have to tell you, Lis? This is about *you* and *me*.' He closes the door of the drinks cabinet quietly behind him. 'Now let's begin again, shall we? This gentleman is going to prepare our will, you and I are going to sign it, and that will be an end to the matter. I'm not asking for much, Lissie. I am simply asking that you help me to die with my affairs in order. Am I not entitled to that modicum of dignity?'

She laughs, girlish and grim all at once. 'Dignity? When will you understand, Jack? Death isn't going to buy you dignity! Your "affairs" will *never* be in order! There have been a few women too many for that!' She swings her crossed leg so energetically, her low-heeled court shoe seems poised to fly off.

'You're talking nonsense, Lissie, and you know it.'

'The sad truth is, I honestly don't know what I know any more.'

Her foot continues to tap out its angry dirge on the air. Mr

Richardson rubs the bridge of his nose, downs the rest of his shot, and turns to the wall.

The will writer sighs – not audibly, he hopes. He waits as long as he dares, then finally closes his case, releases himself from the powerful suck of the sofa and clambers to his feet. What else can he do but reach into his jacket pocket and pass Mr Richardson his card? His last hope. 'I suspect it's best if I leave you for the moment,' he says quietly. He doesn't say he truly wishes it were different. He doesn't say how much he would appreciate the contribution their signed consent from would make to his monthly tally.

'I understand.' Mr Richardson chews the inside of his cheek. 'I'm sorry to have wasted your time.'

'Not at all. Should you require my services again, the office is open from nine till eight daily. You also have my personal mobile number there,' he says, pointing to the fine print.

He crosses the room. 'Mrs Richardson, it was very nice to see you again. I hope I may be of some assistance in the future.' He repeats the well-worn words, though he knows very well there is no future for him here. There won't be another appointment. Mr Richardson will choose to forget that the will writer, the silent witness to his life's mayhem, ever existed.

Mrs Richardson turns. 'Let me see you out.'

'No need, really.'

She smiles her nervous, delicate smile. 'I insist.' She motions him into the hall, passes him his coat, opens the door, and steps into the night. She stands there on the threshold for so long a moment, it almost comes as a surprise to the will writer when she remembers him behind her.

He looks down. She is offering him her hand in spite of the tears sliding down her powdered cheek. 'Good luck with that raffle,' she whispers. 'I'll cross my fingers your number comes up.'

'Thank you.'

'And you'll give my apologies to your wife for keeping you?'

He nods and steps on to the drive, the security light suddenly flooding the night. He hits the central locking, tosses his Your Will briefcase on to the passenger seat and slides across the driver's seat, adjusting the lumbar-support knob. When he looks up, he doesn't expect to see her still at the door, hugging herself against the cold. She stands watching, even as he moves into gear, even as he glides on to the street. She stands watching as if he is driving away with all the luck in the world.

And indeed, the next morning, it is as if Luck herself has climbed into the seat next to him. All the usual bottlenecks are clear. The roadworks have vanished. The car that, according to the Traffic Line, was rear-ended on the A240 slip road has already been recovered. He even arrives at the office early enough to nab a prime parking space.

Yet, in spite of the auspicious start to the day, the will writer's breakfast churns. It's the last Friday in the month. Targets Day. Or 'Name and Shame Day', as it's more commonly known. By ten, ten-thirty at the latest, the monthly completion figures will have been tabulated and the spreadsheet tacked to the Regional Manager's door.

He is hovering by the nearby stationery cupboard when the RM's door opens and his PA appears. A big-boned girl, he recalls. A girl whose broad back and bottom are spreading into an affront as he waits for her to post the sheet and leave; as he anticipates the figures that will confirm his worries have indeed been needless.

At last she walks away in the direction of the call centre. He straightens his tie. He looks to his left and then to his right. There is no one in the immediate vicinity. Nevertheless, he ensures that he is not too quick in his approach. He is, after all, just passing.

Only he does not pass. He does not move on. He does not return to his desk and knock back his second caffeine-hit of the day. He blinks. He rocks slightly on the balls of his feet. He feels his mouth go dry. For the first time in his eighteen-year career, the will writer beholds his name and his figures among the ranks of the lower third. Only the four probationers have performed less illustriously.

And Exeter Man is suddenly behind him – of course he is – tapping the spreadsheet with a stubby finger. 'Now the interesting thing about numbers,' he announces, 'is that they don't lie. People lie, but numbers don't.'

The will writer feels his temples throb, his throat tighten. Say nothing, he tells himself. Say nothing.

And remember – keep remembering – in a world where SUVs have begun to look like their owners, complete with love handles and mushy seats, the H2 proves that there is still one out there that can drop and give you twenty.

Just days till the draw. November 30th. Ticket number 1009.

He is still blinking in front of the one-way glass of the door when it opens and the Regional Manager himself appears. 'A word?' he says.

The will writer nods. 'Certainly.'

'You've seen the figures, I take it?'

'I have.'

The RM motions him towards a plastic chair. 'Problems?'

'No,' he smiles, shaking his head, 'nothing I can't handle.' One of the chair's legs is slightly shorter than the others so the will writer wobbles as he crosses his legs. 'Just a rather erratic month. Too many introductory appointments thrown my way by the call centre and not enough follow-ups.'

'It's up to you to get the follow-ups. You know that.'

'I only meant –'

'We're lowering your targets.' The RM glances at his nails.

'Excuse me?'

'We're lowering your targets.'

'I can hit my targets.'

'You haven't. That's the problem. I'm reducing your road-time by a day a week. Possibly two. Let's see how you manage.'

'Pre-Christmas is always slow. It's the same for everyone. People are, quite simply, too merry.'

'Muslims, too, it would appear.'

The will writer swallows.

'If you meet your revised targets, I'll reassess the situation in a few months.' The RM turns over a sheet on his desk. 'You're fifty-two in February. Is that right?'

'Yes.'

'You haven't considered our early-retirement package?'

'I thoroughly enjoy the job.'

The RM looks up. 'Never too early, I always say, to start investing in your hobbies.'

Like the Hummer Driving Academy. 'On the same course where the US army and Allied Forces have trained drivers, you'll face twisted, muddy terrain . . .' Hasn't he bought the ticket? Isn't he counting down the days?

The will writer sits on the rear of one driver after another most of the way back to Surbiton. Who *are* these people who pull into the outside lane and fail to overtake? He dreams of the chrome grille guard. Once used for pushing oryx out of the road in Namibia, the grille guard, in the urban landscape, adds that final touch of authority, especially when viewed through a rear-view mirror.

He'll opt for the wrap-round variety. 'Made of one-inch-thick tubular steel, its chrome outshines most anything on or off the road.' And he *will* outshine. Exeter Man. The Regional Manager. Sheena and Kirsty and their pitying smiles from over the wall in the call centre.

Make no mistake. He'll shine all right. With Yasmeen there in the passenger seat beside him. With her bracelets tinkling at her pretty wrist. With her English-language CDs playing on the premium digital sound system. With the fresh bouquet awaiting her at home to celebrate. With Michael, his son, already a flutter in her tummy.

Of course he'll shine.

With no memory whatsoever of the day his own slow death began.

Rosie's Tongue

My mother said she should have seen it coming.

At the age of five, I could roll my tongue into a fat little sausage and swallow it whole. By the time I was ten, I could out-twist any tongue-twister while chewing gum at the same time: she was selling seashells down by the seashore faster than it was ever thought possible. And in the schoolyard, in the bite of midwinter, my tongue would glide lickety-split off the frosted metal of the monkey bars while other kids were left dangling by the tips of their tongues. It was when I turned thirteen that my mother said she would have to take me to see Dr Freeman. Things had got out of hand, she said. I couldn't hold my tongue.

Dr Freeman's office was in the five-storey Shopping Village on the main road. While my mother window-shopped our way to the waiting room, I made a mental plan of the nearest exits.

There were none. Only potted plastic palm trees as far as the eye could see.

Dr Freeman's receptionist was wearing a badge on her peach lapel. It read HI! I'M RAQUEL.

'HI, RAQUEL!' I joined in. 'I'M ROSIE!'

Raquel looked up from her appointment book, a little shaken. She had wings of yellow hair that defied gravity. The sight of them made me want to fly. She turned and addressed my mother. 'You can go right through. Dr Freeman's expecting you.'

With her stalwart handbag on one arm, my mother guided me up the narrow corridor with the other. The door was open – I could just see upholstered walls – then it shut without warning.

'Please, have a seat.'

Dr Freeman leaned forward, across his desk, and smiled comfortingly. On the windowsill behind him was a picture of his wife with two slavering Labradors. As I took my seat, I noticed he wore contact lenses that turned his eyes a Technicolor green. He was trying to mesmerize me, and I knew it. So did my mother, but she only looked on, smiling her you-know-best, I-sacrifice-my-only-daughter-to-you smile.

'Rosie,' he began, 'I want you to tell me why you are here.' He hadn't blinked once since we had walked into the room.

I swallowed. 'I – '

'Go on.'

'My mother – '

She stopped smiling. 'That's right, Rosie. Blame it on me. Tell the doctor it's all my . . .' Her words died away. She was wearing half-a-dozen stray rubber bands around her wrists, household finds that were always on the verge of coming in handy. Now she was anxiously twisting a thick red one, threatening her own blood supply.

I slapped her martyred wrist and returned to the doctor. 'My mother says I'm crazy with hormones.' I gave him a flirtatious little wink.

His green eyes didn't so much as flicker. But I heard them say, 'Tell me about your dreams, Rosie.'

I looked away. I wouldn't give in. I took a deep breath. 'Right. Pencil ready? By the time I'm sixteen, I want to be in the Ice Capades. I want to wear one of those little silver skirts, and when I spin, I'll wow the crowd because I won't be wearing any underwear. By the time I'm twenty-one, I want to be a starlet, a heroine with yellow ringlets who wins the hearts of all by tying the hero with the square jaw to the railway tracks. Are you with me? And by the time I'm old, I want to be a grand dame with a mouth full of curses and plenty of cleavage.'

Dr Freeman was tapping the dangerous point of his pencil against his clipboard. 'Rosie,' he said, 'it would seem you deliberately misunderstood me. Shall we try again? I would like you to tell me what you dreamed, say, last night.' The Technicolor green was flashing. I couldn't find my reflection in his eyes. He was making me his own, and my mother's hand at the other end of that thick rubber band was looking blue and lifeless.

'I dreamed . . .'

'Yes, Rosie. I'm listening.'

'Tell the doctor, Rosie.'

'I dreamed I was at the entrance of the twenty-four-hour supermarket where my mother shops by day, but never at night. Never at night.' My voice was slowing down in my head. It was gathering strange echoes. 'My face was pressed to the big glass pane, and the whole store was lit up like some kind of fluorescent heaven. There were people there, too many people for the middle of the night. Something wasn't right. I – I was about to turn away when I realized that everyone was asleep except me. Everyone was sleep-shopping.

'Then the automatic door opened by itself and I walked through. But I was so scared that I was going to wake someone . . .'

'So what did you do, Rosie?'

'I slipped off my loafers so they wouldn't squeak and shelved them with the day-old bread. I was heading for the meat chiller when I saw the butcher with the blood on his apron.'

'Did he see you?'

'No – I'm not sure. You see, I jumped into the arms of a passing stockboy and pretended I was his bride until I was safely past. Then I followed the cold breeze to the meat chiller.'

'What were you looking for, Rosie?'

'I didn't know, not at first. I crept past the lamb chops that bleated at me from the cold, and the chicken silicon breasts. That's when I saw them.'

'Saw what, Rosie? Tell me what you saw.'

'The cows' tongues. I could see them through the clouds of dry ice. They were lying there, silent on those styrofoam trays. Dozens of them. My hand was reaching for one. My mouth was watering. I could feel the blue, wrinkled skin of the cellophane. I picked up the tray. That's when the tip of that tongue began to wriggle and flex. The cellophane started to rip. I tried to seal it up again. I tried to put it back. "They cut out my tongue!" it shrieked. "They called me a silly cow. A silly, silly cow!" The sleep-shoppers were waking up. The butcher was coming my way. I dropped the guilty tongue. I ran back to my stockboy. I jumped into his arms. "Happy Anniversary, sweet stockboy of mine!" I sang.

'That's all.' I looked up. I felt cold. Exposed. I had surrendered to Dr Freeman.

But there was no Dr Freeman. There was no mother. I stood up. I seemed to be alone with only the clipboard on the chair where Dr Freeman had been.

Then I saw them – on all fours in the shag pile. Dr Freeman had dropped one of his contacts. The spell was broken.

'Right, Rosie,' he said with his one green eye, 'I think you've made genuine progress here today. What do you think?'

I stuck out my tongue. I grabbed my mother's handbag, slung it over her arm, and pushed her, sobbing, out of the office, past Raquel, and into the Shopping Village.

It was that night, in my sweet-teen bedroom, that I received the gift of tongues.

The air was still and sticky-hot. The street lights cast bars of light through my Venetian blinds and across my bare arms and legs. I lay awake, listening to the blue electric sizzle of mosquitoes as they hit the bug-killer in our backyard. I couldn't sleep. I rolled over, twice. I pulled the sheet up, then off again. I turned myself wrong-side up, so that my feet rested on my pillow and my head lolled over the end of the bed I had outgrown. Blood rushed to my face. A bar of light caught me across the eyes and shattered into purple and gold as I closed them. I was thirsty. My tongue felt thick in my mouth. I thought about the glass of stale water on my night table, up at the other end of the bed, but I never made it. Before I could shift my feet from the pillow, I was bolt upright in bed and charged like a lightning rod. My spine was rigid; my jaw, locked.

I waited – for I don't know how long – my fists gripping the sheet. I waited for the awful hush that filled me up to break, to crack open, to let go of me. Something was pushing and swelling in the dark of my throat, and I was scared.

Part of me was saying, this isn't happening – a ghost of a voice inside my head that I could hardly hear. It was saying, whatever this is, it doesn't happen in the suburbs. I could hear a dog barking a few streets away, but I couldn't turn my head. I could hear the thrum of traffic from the distant highway, but I couldn't swallow. I wasn't myself. Not at all. And if I wasn't myself, who was I?

From the corner of my eye, I could just make out something in my bedroom mirror. Something flickering, purple and orange and yellow and blue. It was a single tongue of fire, sitting on the darkness like an optical illusion. For a moment, I forgot about everything: the sizzle of the mosquitoes and the charge between my vertebrae and the fearsome silence in my mouth. I just watched that wavering tongue of fire. It had started off small, but it was growing, feeding on the still air. It was the size of a fire-eater's meal when I smelled hair, my hair, burning. That flame was hovering just over my head.

I grabbed my pillow. That's what I remember next – my arms moving again, and my voice yelling 'Fire!', and the power of my own voice almost winding me. But the fire wouldn't be put out.

The fire chief told my father we were lucky. 'Mostly smoke damage,' he said. 'Could have been worse.'

My father was still rubbing his eyes. He looked like a man trapped in someone else's dream. 'How did it happen?'

'Well, we're investigating, sir, but if you want my opinion . . .'

'Please.'

'Looks to me like a case of a faulty teenage girl. Somewhere I'd say between the ages of twelve and sixteen. I've seen it before.'

I left the shelter of the garage where my mother and I huddled in our nightgowns. I ran into the driveway, pushing myself between father and fire chief. 'That's me,' I breathed. 'The girl.' My father hardly looked at me. It was all too clear who I was. 'I can explain every –'

'You gotta be careful,' said the fire chief, ignoring me. 'They're touchy as touchpaper at this age.'

'But it wasn't like that!' I cried.

Breakfast was burned toast and sausages. My mother was crying again. My father told her it was time for the priest.

It was cramped in the confessional, but my mother insisted. She stood with her back against the door and prompted me.

'Forgive me, Father, for I have sinned,' I repeated.

'Yes, Rosie,' came the voice of Father Pater from the other side of the mouldering velvet curtain. There was no such thing as anonymity in our town. 'What is it you would like to confess?'

Silence.

And more silence. My mother kicked my ankle.

'I stink of smoke. Three guesses.'

'I did hear about the fire last night. Were you smoking in bed again?'

I hesitated. 'Do you want the truth, Father?'

'Naturally.'

My mother bit her lip.

'I received the gift of tongues. Pentecostally speaking, that is.'

'I see.'

He didn't. I could tell. The air in the confessional was stale and warm. Sweat gathered on my forehead. I tried to breathe. 'There was a flame, above my head. And my voice, it was big, in my throat.'

'A flame, you say?'

'Yes, Father.'

Father Pater inhaled loudly. He was taking my air. 'Well, if that was the case, do you know what this means, Rosie?'

'No – no – I don't.' I was starting to hyperventilate.

'It means hellfire. It just might mean possession. In short, it means you've been a naughty girl.'

'And her penance, Father?' asked my mother, chiming in.

'Well, it's debatable, of course, but I've always said, mortify the flesh, save the soul.'

'BUT I'M STILL DEVELOPING!' I screamed. I clambered to my feet and heaved on the door, sending my mother flying into the pile of hymnals outside. A pair of altar boys whistled as I ran out of the church, gulping for air.

I ran and I ran as fast as I could. I ran until I made it to Buddy's Ice Cream Parlour on the edge of town. Buddy Junior, who lived on the wrong side of the old railway tracks, was scooping ice cream.

'Make it a double, Buddy,' I panted.

'Sure thing, Rosie.' I watched his muscle scurry up and down his arm as he carved out two scoops of Chocolate Sin. He smiled at me through the glass. 'You're looking really hot today, Rosie.'

'I ran all the way here.'

'Glad to hear it. This one's on the house.'

I smiled back and took a seat on one of the spinning stools at the counter. Then I licked my cone clear way round its creamy circumference. Buddy leaned across the counter. 'Nice to see you again, Rosie.'

I went on licking my cone. He couldn't take his eyes off my tongue.

'Talk to me, Rosie.'

'Maybe I will. Maybe I won't. But I'm not saying anything, Buddy, until I finish this cone.'

'But, Rosie,' he sulked, 'it's a friggin' double whammy.'

I licked a dollop of chocolate off the end of my nose with the tip of my tongue. I finished in my own good time. Then I spun round languorously on my stool a few times. At last I said, 'The truth is, Buddy, I'm all talked out. Why don't you just go ahead and kiss me.'

Buddy hurdled the counter, and it's true. My tongue was a wonder in his mouth. It moved like no other. It ran circles round his. It did somersaults, backwards and forwards. For a little while, it danced the rumba. Then it disappeared in a game of hide-and-seek. Finally, it reappeared and did a loop-the-loop in mid-air. Buddy was the first boy I'd met who could hold his breath for as long as me.

We might have been there for hours if my mother hadn't walked in. 'Rosie, you will take your tongue out of that boy's mouth this instant!'

Buddy leaped back over the counter and hid.

'How could you, Rosie? How could you just run off like that?' She took a seat on the stool next to mine, spinning dolefully. For a time, neither of us spoke. Then my mother let out a great sigh and slumped over the Formica counter. 'Rosie, I have not said this yet, but I am saying it now. I am at a loss. I am at an absolute loss. You have stuck your tongue out at a doctor. You have set fire to your father's house. You have bedevilled our parish priest. How, Rosie – can you tell me this? – *how* do you expect me to go on shopping in this town?'

I said I didn't know. Buddy appeared from behind the milk-shake machine and said he didn't know either. My mother and I spun on our stools for a little while longer. There was nothing for it. I'd have to concede something. 'Mom, we can wear our mother-and-daughter sweaters again on Sundays. Would that make you happy?'

'No, Rosie, that will not make me happy. It's too late for our sweaters now. I just want – and this is all I want – I just want you to learn to hold that tongue of yours till you're twenty-one. Is that really too much to ask?'

I looked at my mother's pressed lips.

I looked at Buddy Junior's wide worried eyes.

'No,' I replied, my tongue discovering my cheek, 'of course not, Mother.'

Life and Soul

After Sam Taylor-Wood's *Third Party*

We met in the uncompanionable darkness of Sam Taylor-Wood's *Third Party*.

I knew no one. I had not been to the first party or to the second. Had there been a first or a second? Or was time trapped on Taylor-Wood's flickering video loop? I was about to leave the gallery – I wanted daylight, air, I remember that – when I turned and found myself standing before the oracular, wall-to-wall face of Marianne Faithfull.

Her lipstick was wrong, make no mistake: a burgundy matte gone dry. Beneath it, her lips were a fissured landscape. Her mouth – how many feet wide across the wall? – was parched and lean. An abandoned place. Badlands. No wonder she did not speak. No wonder she kept her own counsel.

She knew better. She watched. She sipped wine. Might it have been then that I noticed you? For already you were there, an inadvertent party-goer in the humming, chattering expanse of the room. *Toujours déjà*. It is difficult to think back. I remember the dark gravity of Faithfull's gaze, its ancient pull. And I remember she stared through me, as if it were I, and not she, who wasn't really there.

Modern art, eh. Snort, snort. Or *sheesh*, as the Americans say. *Sheesh*.

Overhead the lenses of the many projectors stared into the darkness, unearthly as the myriad eyes on an Old Testament angel's wing. I tried to look above, beyond. The ceiling was low.

Too low. (And getting lower? Why hadn't I noticed?) Which is why the air was stale. Which is why my breath was shallow. Could I ask the gallery attendant for a paper bag?

The party. Return to the party. There is every reason to celebrate. To be part of something and not nothing.

I stared at the girl with the swingy hair who – famously now, I believe – would not stop dancing. By herself. For herself. It has to be said she scared me, like clockwork toys and escalators and the spinning wheels of fallen bikes scared me as a child. I turned away and, like you, was drawn to the familiar haunt of the smouldering ashtray. A video mirage, like everything else. We were among ghosts, and here, at this house party, the ghosts were bolder, more self-possessed, than either you or I.

You were no good at small talk. You should have talked about the Millennium Bridge, like everyone else on the South Bank that day; how it had swayed in the high winds like a ramshackle fairground ride on your way over the river. Were they going to close it again? you might have wondered. You should have wondered. But commonplace decencies eluded you.

– Or the Eye. Why did you not ask me if I had been up on the Eye? Perhaps I had seen the advert with the car in that pristine capsule at the very top of London's night sky? We might have mutually conceded its sixty-second glamour. One of us might have mentioned Baudrillard, the loss of the Real. The other need only have nodded. Paper-heart kindness. We might then have gone our own way.

Instead you told me how the universe might suddenly turn inside out, how a black wave might sweep over the world. I could barely see you. You had to be either a paranoid depressive or a Christian fundamentalist. But I listened anyway. Your voice had a discordant music in it, and here, at the party, there was only the usual, urgent futility of spent words. Literally, a soundtrack already familiar.

It was unimaginable, you said. You'd read about it in the *Independent*. News out of CERN. 'The electrical force of the world that we take entirely for granted,' you said, 'might suddenly give way. The whole universe could just switch off.'

'Wonders never,' I said. Next to you, I was cool, composed. I needed you to stay.

'You don't understand. Everything – Big Ben, the sun, the moon, me, you – could go dark.'

'But not before the Jubilee, surely.' At a party, I was the urbane woman in the little black dress, like the one behind me who wanted to have it off with that ginger-haired actor whose name I could never remember.

'You think I'm off my head.'

'You don't have what my mother would call a sunny disposition.'

'I haven't explained things very well.'

'Perhaps not.' I reached for the cigarette resting on the ashtray's brim. My hand came away, disappointed, as it does when your Tube ticket is eaten by the station's exit machine.

'Every particle of matter has a heavier "dark" counterpart. Try imagining yourself recast in pure darkness. I'm not joking. A swap could happen at any point in the vacuum of the universe.'

'And spread.' I wasn't stupid. That much I'd have you know.

'Exactly. Like a rip in the fabric of matter.'

I wanted then to grab your hand. Where *had* matter gone? Had you noticed too? Is that why you were talking like a social misfit? In here, in here we were no longer solid. The *Third Party* was a slow, inconsequential death but a surprisingly easy one, and I realized I didn't want to leave. Chit-chat and half-lies made small rubble behind us, and I wanted to pick my way through it. To mix. To mingle. Was the dark, brutish man on the Conran sofa staring at me? Was it Ray Winstone? Was it a Conran sofa?

You were still talking, I realized. You were saying you

didn't have much longer. Here in the gallery? In London? Time was running out apparently. I'd missed something, a transitional sentence between the cosmos and you.

You were terminal.

Suddenly I felt drunk. I assumed cancer. I had to ask you to repeat it.

'I won't see another party.'

Lord. You were gauche. Burdensome. Who would do this to a complete stranger? 'My God. I'm so sorry,' I said. I wanted to go back to the party.

I was the first person you had told. Yet you didn't know my name. You couldn't have sworn to the colour of my eyes or hair. Was the elegant woman in the black dress actually *with* Ray Winstone? Could she be? Or were they only sleeping together? Who would have thought? I blinked. I tried to focus. You were telling me how you'd struggled to believe it wasn't a failure. You knew it was out of your control, yet you felt you'd let yourself down. You'd realized too late, you said. For treatment, I said. It was the knowing, you said. That was the hardest, I said. Completing your sentences like this, like a lover, made me brave. I touched your sleeve – a gesture from a film.

You were still coming to terms with it all. That's why you'd come here, to the *Third Party*. That's why you hadn't been able to leave. 'Couldn't death be to life,' you said, 'what negative space is to a piece of art? Do you see? Couldn't it be something and not nothing?'

I glanced over my shoulder. I needed a glass of wine.

'The space is the thing, not simply the art. Here, we have what looks like gallery-floor space. Of course, it also looks like standing room for this unbearable house party, so we the viewers are also, we are to understand, party-goers. There is an immediate collapse of the textual and the extra-textual. Which of course we are wise to.'

I forced a smile. I'd been trapped by the party bore. Yet I didn't leave. I didn't lose myself to the shadows. In the dark, you smelled of roll-ups and Persil.

'But all this emptiness is about more than that. It says there *is* a beyond – something beyond, not only the work of art, but, by implication, also the art of life. It says there is something beyond our futile efforts to know the beyond. Do you see?'

'Yes, of course.'

You were ransacking your intelligence. You needed affirmation. How could I tell a dying stranger, this is it, baby? This is all there is. Get used to it. Stop talking. You don't have time to waste.

You had been here all day, in this room, at the empty heart of this eternal ten-minutes of party. No one had asked you to move on. No one, you said, even seemed to know you were here. And, almost in spite of myself, against my better judgement, against type, my hand found yours. My hand found yours even as Faithfull raised her glass – not to us – her eyes smudged and inscrutable over its rim.

As we lay down to make love, I worried fleetingly for the many coats that were not, in fact, beneath us.

'Is she still watching?' I could feel the buttresses of your ribs yield to my breasts and breath. Did I weigh too much? Did you like a woman on top?

'She watches everyone,' you said.

'Have you always wanted that? You know – someone watching.'

'No.' I could barely see you in the flickering dark.

'A public space then?'

'No.'

'My breasts are small.'

'Yes.'

'Schoolgirls? Britney? That video? This blouse? Is that what this is about?'

'Why are you so nervous?'

'You've taken off all your clothes.' But I let myself rest my cheek against your goosepimpled chest.

'That's nice.'

I started to relax. 'Why are we doing this?'

'Because I told you the world will turn off?'

'A line. I've heard better.'

'Because no one's said we can't? Shift down.'

'I mean, do we even like each other?'

'Better. Couldn't say. But *dis*liking someone is, arguably, a neglected form of intimacy.'

'You dislike me?'

'No. Is that nice . . . ?'

'Yes.'

'With my hand?'

'The heel of your hand is better.'

'Take off your skirt.'

'Now?'

'When if not now?'

'Some time we don't find ourselves on the floor of the Hayward Gallery.'

Your hand moved under my M&S knickers. 'You're beautiful.'

'You can hardly see me.'

'Inside then. You're beautiful inside.'

I didn't want to ask. Did you mean beautiful inside as in beautiful in spirit – had you gleaned something rare in the darkness between us? Or did you mean *inside* inside? Did you mean the negative space of me?

I didn't know then that the distinction was a false one. Surface, spirit. Spirit, surface. I am not used to an undivided world. There is so much I must unlearn.

We fell asleep in a far corner, under the shifting blanket of your clothes, under the concrete roof of the world, the projectors' hum a thin memory of some music of the straining spheres.

'Ssshhh,' I said to you once more, 'ssshhh,' though neither of us in fact spoke; though you, by then, already understood: that, too soon, we would renounce even language.

Life, a full life, is arrived at by a series of small deaths. This was the first. The coldness of my skin. The jack-in-the-box jolt of you. Love, the old seizure – I had to remember to breathe.

There aren't the words.

Or, there are no longer.

I'm restless in my sleep. I thrash. I tell you, it was like touching the skin of the world.

You awakened to the vision of me sitting upright, somnolent, my arm outstretched like a terrible divining rod.

Nothing was different. The party was not over. The dancing girl still danced. The couple still flirted. Ray Winstone still brooded. The voices of the other party-goers were like the ocean in a shell.

'It doesn't matter,' you were saying. 'Forget it.'

You knew. You had always known. For the first time, my eyes were accustomed to the attenuated dark. I was staring at my own hand, its palms and fingers flat against the membrane of the world. 'Dear God.'

I was touching some kind of screen. My palm was pressed flat against the wrong side of a screen.

I heard your voice, as if you were already lost to the past: 'I'm sorry,' you said.

You'd deceived me.

You would never have told me that the vanity was mine. Not the flirting woman's. Not the ginger-haired actor's. Not the girl's, dancing for all to see. Not the Ray Winstone character's, so assured he deserved sex this long night. How could I have known it was not I who beheld them, but rather they who'd simply never noticed me?

What would you have said anyway? How could you have

explained that I was the woman who was invisible? The woman at the party whom people look past. The woman who had long ago ceased to turn heads. And you, for your sins, were that woman's lover.

You'd been waiting for me. Were meant for me. It was Fate. Destiny writ large. On my own, a single woman of an uncertain age, I was a loose thread. A flaw in the design. An asymmetry. Together, on the other hand, you and I were that necessarily unremarkable thing: the couple people would never remember. Extras.

Except now we were naked. At a house party. From somewhere, I could make out a barely suppressed joke. The ginger-haired actor was laughing. Even I knew: none of this was supposed to be happening. We'd broken with Fate: we'd been noticed.

I wanted to shout at everyone, 'Leave us alone! He's got cancer, for God's sake!' as if that explained anything. But you stopped me. You held me fast in your arms. Knowledge was snapping at my heels. Of course, you didn't have cancer. That wasn't it at all.

'That feeling,' I started, 'that feeling that I'm not quite . . . that I can't ever remember feeling real –'

'Is real,' you said.

And you smiled, gently. I could just see the line of your mouth, the glow of your teeth. You wanted to comfort me, but your teeth frightened me. Were they false or did they only look false?

You were pulling your jacket over my shoulders, covering my nakedness, as Adam might have done had he found Eve in a patio garden in London instead of Paradise. I had gone so cold. 'Ssshhh,' you said. 'Ssshhh.'

'We're nothing.'

'We're not nothing.'

'What is "not nothing"? What does "not nothing" mean?'

You got hold of me. Your thumbs hurt my shoulders. 'It means me and you. Us . . . before. Together like that. That was not nothing.'

'When did I arrive? When did I join the party?' I was as egotistical as a child.

'You are always arriving.'

'Yet I never learn?'

'It's hard.'

'You knew.'

'I always seem to know – about the world, about it switching off. It's just another loop. It means I'm the perpetual killjoy, the one nobody wants to find themselves in a corner with.'

'So just as I'm always arriving, you're always leaving. You're always on your way out. Always terminal. Which means – my God, do you see? – which means you're not really leaving me at all. We're okay. You're right. We're okay. This is a loop, after all.'

'Not any more it's not.'

'Don't you see? You're always saying that. You always feel that. But you always come back.'

'No, things are different this time. And that's not just the pessimism talking – which is precisely the problem. My pessimism is gone.'

'How can you be so sure?'

'Everything's changed. *I've* changed.'

'Not everything. Never everything. Don't go hyperbolic on me.'

'You took my hand. For the first time, you took my hand.'

I glance back nervously at the party. 'No one saw. No one was looking.'

'Can't you see? I'm happy. I'm actually *happy*.'

'You're not happy. It's not in you to be happy. You're glad. You feel warm. You feel temporarily comforted. A little light-headed. This is a good spell. Believe me, you are not happy.'

'I'm happy. I have been since –'

'Since I took your hand.' I scanned the room for exits. Where were the exit signs? 'I'm afraid,' I said.

'Me too.'

'You won't be back.'

'No,' you said quietly. 'It's impossible. I'm not the man I was.'

'I can't bear it.'

'You'll know no different.'

'Something in me will.'

'We'll see – You'll see.'

'All that stuff, about the world turning off. It wasn't just the paranoia talking, was it?'

You closed your eyes against the tears.

'Don't,' I said.

'Don't what?' you said.

'Despair.'

'Why not?'

'Because I can't comfort you. Everything's changed, except me. I'm as weak, as frightened as ever. You shouldn't have fallen for someone like me. All I can really think about is myself, how much I'm afraid of the dark. How, at home, wherever home is or was, I have night lights in every socket –'

'I'll hold you. When it happens, I'll hold on.'

'I have to tell you something. If the Ray Winstone character had noticed me, I might have gone off with him. Do you know that? I don't deserve your love. Do you remember Julia and Winston? At the end, do you remember how –'

'Ssssh . . .'

We were quiet for a long time. We did not bother to dress. We adopted the carelessness of exiles. I said I was worried I'd forgotten to unplug the iron before leaving my flat that afternoon, and we laughed. I said I could even tell you the brand name, and we laughed harder. If Faithfull hadn't suddenly looked up, her seer's eyes trained on the beyond, her sibyl's mouth taut, we would not have known. We did not hear the footsteps. We did not see the technicians in black.

We watched the eyes of the projectors go out, one by one, like dying stars. 'Wish,' you said. 'Wish.' You didn't want me to see the other party-goers as they blinked into unbeing: first the dancing girl, then the flirting couple, then Ray Winstone. He looked relieved, glad to be released at last from the weight of his own unhappiness, from the undertow of his drives; glad to be no more.

I saw the ashtray disappear.

My last glimpse was not of you, I confess, but of Faithfull. She yawned. All of a sudden. Did you see it too? Her mouth gaped into a hole, and I understood. Here was the first rip in the fabric of the world.

You took me in your arms. I pushed my face into your chest. I heard the humming of the spheres go quiet. I felt the crashing of your heart go still, even as the light went out in me, cell by cell, photon by photon. The Old Testament wing had come down upon us, dark and vast as love.

I speak to you. In the wide ocean of my thoughts, between the black waves. In the quietude that has no horizons.

Will Taylor-Wood throw another party? A fourth party? (Was there a first? Was there a second?) You will not be there to take my wrap, or pass me a glass of punch, or light my cigarette. Do not worry. I have no illusions. I am no longer afraid.

Hear me. I'll be the one alone at the ashtray, the life and soul.

Radiant Heat

'No warmth is lost in the universe'
Hildegard of Bingen

Ron McLelland drives for IGA's food fleet. Mostly meat and dairy. Sometimes, fresh produce. Once, in a crazy kamikaze mission, oranges from Florida and back again to Halifax in three days. He'd called his wife, Linda, from a payphone beside a take-out place shaped like a giant burger on a bun and he'd tried to describe to her twilight in the Everglades: the stink of the swamps; the wind moving like a ghost through the sawgrass; the weird calls of waders he couldn't see in the gathering dark. He said it made him think about what it must be like to die alone, and she said, what's with men always brooding on their own mortality? Hadn't she told him all those caffeine pills would give him the jitters?

Ron is one of six IGA drivers who have volunteered. He's been allocated a twenty-eight-foot refrigeration trailer, made for long haul. He sits in his cab reading Friday's *Daily News*, waiting for the programming instructions. On page 3, a waitress at the Sou'Wester Restaurant is predicting doom for the local lobster catch. 'People just won't feel right,' she says. 'Not now they won't. Well, they're scavengers, lobsters, aren't they?'

He throws the paper to the floor of the cab. For a moment, unaccountably, he feels something choking the back of his throat, like the time his brother Neil made him pay ten cents to see a picture of Marilyn Monroe almost naked, and there it was, in grisly black and white, her bloated body on an autopsy table.

The call comes through from the depot. Minus twenty, they say. 'Ron? That's minus twenty.' Deep freeze.

Long-haulage was Ron's solution to death, the family business. For him, it had long been an unfortunate point of familial pride that, in April 1912, his grandfather James McLelland – then a twenty-year-old completing an apprenticeship at John Snow & Co. Undertakers – had been one of the team aboard the *MacKay-Bennett* the morning she left port with the tons of ice, the lengths of canvas, the embalmers' tools and the hundred coffins.

They'd spotted the berg itself – you couldn't miss it – a two-hundred foot twin-peaked mountain of ice. 'Imagine it,' James McLelland would say to Ron and Neil over his saucer of tea. 'It was like God Himself coming at you. Not angry, just indifferent, which, I promise you, is by far the worse. I saw plenty of growlers out there too, the small bergs that hide in the swell, the ones that can hole your hull as easily as you two crunch an apple, but I'm telling you, I never seen the likes of that berg.'

In the span of just three days, the bodies had drifted almost fifty miles from the coordinates the captain had been given. That much they could tell the papers. 'Of course, what none of us could say is that we hit some of the bodies, there were that many. We knocked 'em clean out of the water, five, six feet into the air. It was like something out of a crazy cartoon. You couldn't believe it was happening.

'When we dropped anchor at last, the weird thing was, most of them looked like they'd only nodded off. That's what we said. 'Cause of course they were frozen upright in the jackets – lot of good those things were. Just made for a slower death. And, Lord, what a mess. A terrible wreath it was all around the hull. Bodies, limbs, wreckage, pack ice . . . I can still see this woman in her nightdress clasping a baby to her breast. A Cape Breton lad called Pat Mundy had to jump from clamper to clamper to reach her with one of the hooks, long-jumping those floes like he did as a boy for fun in North Sydney Harbour. Couldn't reach her. Nor the three men beside her, all of them clinging to the same chair.

'We buried a hundred and sixteen at sea in burlap bags weighted with iron: all of them bodies damaged during the sinking, or smashed in the ice floe, or eaten by sea creatures. First-class passengers, of course, we embalmed and put in coffins, no matter how bad they looked.

'Problem was, after only four days, we run out of the embalming fluid. The captain, he contacts the White Star Line's New York office; says they have to send more supplies and a second ship. As it was, the best we could do for the steerage folk was to wrap them up in canvas; and for the crew, to lay them out on the deck, covered with tarps. With the wind at night and the ship wallowing on the rollers, you could have sworn they were breathing still, poor devils.

'Three hundred and six bodies. That was the cargo.'

The day after Ron's thirteenth birthday, James McLelland himself would be waked, open casket, in the Serenity Room of McLelland & Sons Family Funeral Home. He would wear on his face the taut cosmetic expression of unwrinkled peace that had been his own point of professional pride. He would never know that only five years on, his eldest grandson, Ron, would fail his exams. All of them. Pathology. Restorative Art. Funeral Rites. Mortuary Law. Embalming Theory and Practice. Merchandising and Management. He would not dream that, at the age of eighteen, Ron would boast nothing more than a high-school diploma and a heavy-goods driving licence. 'And how far do you think that's going to get you in this day and age, Ron?' Ron's dad, James's son, shouted over the smashed body of a thirty-year-old father of three. 'You tell me that.'

'Far,' said Ron, his chest heaving. 'Far from here.'

When Kurt arrives at JFK Airport, his flight number is already flashing on the monitors. The baggage belts have broken down. The line at the check-in doubles and redoubles on itself. Children sleep on soft-sided matching luggage. Middle-aged men rest their paunches on abandoned ticket counters. He feels he's walked into a B-movie where the population is in the grip of the dreaded E-Force. 'E', a dome-headed scientist will explain to his frightened but winsome technician, 'is for "Entropy",' and she will duly scream.

'Excuse me, bitte,' Kurt says, faltering loudly. 'Excuse me. My wife is, right now, yes, a baby having in Geneva. The plane leaves. Excuse me –' He moves slowly up the line, blushing at the success of the lie.

'Hey, bub.' Something thumps his arm. He stops short, turns around. A stocky man hidden behind tinted glasses and sideburns from 1976 reaches into his breastpocket. Kurt steps back. Air rage. This is where it all begins. 'See this?' Kurt looks down. A fat Cuban cigar. 'No, don't thank me, just name the kid after me – Max, since you're not asking.' Someone slaps him on the back as he clambers over a barrier. An elderly woman thrusts a box of brandy-filled chocolates under his arm. 'For your wife,' she says, squeezing his hand. Before he knows it, he's at the check-in desk. He loves Americans.

A blonde in a crisp blue blazer reaches for his documents. 'Thank you, Dr Zucker. You want gate 21. The last one.' She leans across the desk and smiles. 'So leg it.'

He sprints, laptop and portable CD player banging at his hip. He clears the gate, nods sheepishly to the stewardess, and falls into his seat aboard the Boeing MD-11 at six minutes past eight in the evening, only ten minutes before take-off.

'I see you've noticed my socks.' It's his neighbour in 18A. He nods to his bright purple feet, wriggling his toes. 'Before you ask, I'm not Donny Osmond. Let's clear that up right away.'

Kurt nods, fumbles for his CD player, loads it with Bowie's *Young Americans* as the plane begins to taxi down the runway.

'So what takes you to Geneva? Sorry. Didn't get your name.'

'Kurt. A conference. At CERN.' A steward stops and reminds

him to turn off the CD player for take-off. There is no escape after all.

'Kurt? Hal. I've heard of that. Quantum foam, right?'

'Right.'

'You giving a paper, Kurt?'

'Yes.'

'Got a title?'

'Yes, but –'

'Go on.'

' "Thermalization in Ultrarelativistic Heavy Ion Collisions. Subtitle: Energy Densities and Entropy Production." '

'It's got a ring to it.'

Kurt smiles wanly. The conversation dies.

His passion is particle accelerators – the generation of high-energy systems. In the lab at Brookhaven, he bears witness to explosions of heat and light that have not been possible since the early days of the universe. But there's more to it than that because privately, deeply, irrationally, Kurt Zucker struggles against the Second Law of Thermodynamics. Against the tyranny of entropy.

On the armrest, Hal's arm is warm against his.

A young fisherman called Ian shares hot tea from his thermos. He's telling Ron that the exclusion zone goes on for ever. His father, he says, went out early on Thursday, 'bout three in the morning. 'The whole bay is glowing yellow from the flares, right? And the phone starts ringing and my old man says he's going. Won't let me go. But in less than an hour, he's back, you know, peeling off the oilskins. "Can't do it," he's saying. "It's wreckage out there. Just wreckage," and I know he means he's found no one, no one alive. He looks at me and his eyes are filling up. "I don't know what to do," he says. "Don't go back, Dad," I says. "The military, they're here." "You don't understand," he says. "I got a piece of a woman in the boat. A piece of a woman." '

Ian and Ron are standing on the bright sweep of ancient granite that disappears in a reef under the rim of St Margaret's Bay. They can smell jet fuel on the wind. Past the lighthouse, breakers crash like the backs of breaching whales.

'Can't be easy for them divers,' says Ian. Ron shakes his head, zips up his jacket all the way to his Adam's apple. There's been rain. High winds. Two-metre swells. They're down there, he thinks, at sixty metres, on tethers, the water close to freezing – that's what one of the guys was telling him at the makeshift canteen. They're in weighted boots so they can stand up on the seabed, because it's not flat like you imagine. It's grey slate lined with ridges and deep valleys. It's studded with granite boulders that loom up sudden. Visibility is only a few metres. 'A nightmare,' the diver told Ron.

At Friday noon, the head of the salvage operation will stand in the parking lot of the Sou'Wester Restaurant and confirm for the world media that the plane hit the water so violently it shattered into more than a million pieces.

John Campbell stares into a rock pool while a reporter from Toronto questions him. She thinks him shy, an old bachelor who can't look a woman in the eye. 'That's all,' he says, patiently: he was watching the *Titanic* video by himself at home when he heard an almighty boom of thunder. 'A double thump,' he says, 'like the sound Concorde makes when it breaks the sound barrier over the Bay every morning. Except this time, the beams in my house shook.'

'A double thump?' she says.

'Yes.'

'Like a heartbeat.' She makes a note.

He wants her to go away. 'They're doing coffee and tea in the vestry, you know,' He doesn't want her to see the baby's shoe floating in the rock pool.

Brenda Murphy is about to be interviewed in St John's Church by a middle-aged man in an Armed Forces uniform. They loiter by the church portals, looking out towards the brooding Bay.

'Well,' he says at last.

'Yes,' she sighs.

He motions her into the crying room. There is a wooden desk on which schoolchildren have etched their names, and two chairs. He looks not at her but at a humming laptop screen as she gives her name, address and place of work. She feels the words-to-be jangling within her. She looks at this man, at the dark hair that springs from the gaps between his buttons, and she despairs that he is not enough; that neither of them is enough.

On Wednesday night, she was in her mobile home at New Harbour Point. She opened the door at ten-thirty to let out Lucky, her dog, when she saw something, about 300 yards across the Bay. 'At first it was a light like I'd never seen,' she says. 'I thought, isn't that beautiful. You see,' she adds, blushing, 'there was a lot of mist out here, so the whole sky was glowing with it. For a moment, I wondered if maybe it wasn't a dying firework behind the cloud cover. Or a meteor maybe. Everything was luminous, and, it's funny, but I felt almost luminous myself with it. You don't think, do you? By the time I spotted the flames, it was falling into the Bay.'

Ginny told Kurt she wasn't going to wait for their marriage to burn out when he did. He said, 'We'll have a baby. Soon.' She said, what did he expect her to conceive with – a turkey-baster? He had energy, brio, charm, maverick wit – all of the above – for his colleagues, for his students. Then he returned to her, spent, cold.

And she felt isolated in Hamburg. Hamburg made her ridiculous. Irrational. It made her cry after lunch at his mother's. It made her sicken for no reason at the sight of the small scar on his mother's face, visible through the heavy beige matte of her foundation. It made her start wondering what Kurt's family had got up to – had really got up to – during the war. His father had been a leading chemist. Could one suddenly turn up as a leading chemist in 1949? And hadn't Kurt's grandfather or great-grandfather been a phrenologist? Wasn't that just steps away from eugenics? Could she propagate such a line?

It made her crave American TV. After work, she watched more and more, an overzealous observer of bad dubbing, angrier each time at the incongruity of lips. These days, she told Kurt, she felt badly dubbed herself. Her voice seemed to slow in her head as she spoke, as if some inner clockwork was running down.

Kurt does not take a complimentary newspaper or the duty-free list. He does not watch the security video on the overhead monitor. He strips the small white pillow of its plastic case, leans his head back, and remembers, in spite of himself, the first time Ginny flew back to the States for Christmas, leaving him in Hamburg. He slept every night with his face buried in her nightdress. Four years later, who were they? She returned each day from the circulation desk smelling of yellowing books – a vomit-like smell he remembered from school textbooks. He'd never wanted sex less. She had never been so broody. She moved sluggishly. She was putting on weight. When the offer came for the residency in New York, he thought it was the answer. She said, what was the point? He'd never come home there either.

DESY, his employer, agreed the release to the lab at Brook-haven – so he started life anew in her home town. She remained in his. They agreed separation, anti-climactically, weeks later by long distance. They discussed practicalities. They confirmed they'd see other people. That was what separation meant.

Kurt opens one eye. The beverage cart is trundling its way down the aisle. He thinks about phoning Ginny on the in-flight phone. He imagines waking her from sleep; telling her he is speaking to her from ten thousand feet and rising. He imagines her voice warm, drowsy, unguarded: 'Head in the clouds? Not you,' she says, smiling through a yawn. He wonders whether he can say, casually enough, 'Maybe I'll hop a flight from Geneva to Hamburg. Can you get a day off?' He is digging for a credit card when Hal looks up from the pocket security card and smiles broadly. It can wait, Kurt tells himself.

Across the aisle, the stewardess is speaking to John and Joan, from Eugene, Oregon. Joan is in her mid-sixties. He's maybe ten years older. She orders a vodka with cranberry juice and thanks the stewardess for the extra blanket. 'Do you know,' Joan says, 'we last travelled to Europe together for our honeymoon twenty-five years ago? We'd each been widowed the year before; were both travelling on business. I worked for the Democrats then. John was in ladies' hosiery – sorry, honey. He *owned* a ladies' hosiery wholesalers – she knew what I meant. We met on a plane travelling out of Minneapolis. I'm sentimental about it,' she says, 'but John hates flying as much as ever, don't you, honey?'

'A Scotch, please,' he barks at the stewardess.

Kurt has been trying not to stare at the stewardess's brochure-face as she guides the stubborn drinks cart down the aisle. He tries to stop looking through the fresh white cotton of her blouse at the outline of her bra. He does not want to succumb to cliché. He is bored. That's the problem. Hal has had the window blind lowered since take-off.

'After you, Kurt,' says Hal, lowering his meal tray. The stewardess is standing, attentive, above them. She has a small mole on her right cheek.

'Thanks,' smiles Kurt. 'A white wine, please.'

'French or German, sir?'

'French.'

She selects a wine glass from a compartment in her cart. She unpeels a bottle top with a flick of her long nails and unscrews the lid. He lowers his tray.

'Kurt, don't take this the wrong way,' says Hal, suddenly staring at him, 'but you've got one mega case of hair static. It's airline pillows, right? Synthetic fibres. Get you every time. Just be grateful you've still got hair to stand on end.'

The stewardess is waiting, glass poised in hand. She smiles

politely at him. But her eyes, Kurt thinks, are amused. He feels very short seated so far below her. He raises a hand and tries to flatten his hair without obvious self-consciousness. 'Here, Kurt,' says Hal, 'allow me.' Hal turns, raising his left arm to Kurt's head even as Kurt reaches for the glass. There is a collision of limbs. The glass falls, shattering on Kurt's tray.

'Whoa!' says Hal. John and Joan twist in the seats. Kurt spreads his legs quickly, to avoid the cascade of wine. The stewardess is quick with towels and apologies. 'I'm fine,' he says, helping her to collect the glass shards. Hal orders a Coke and shuts up. Kurt does not return to his CD player. His hand clenches their shared armrest. Hal cedes it to him.

Kurt has in fact forgotten Hal. He has even forgotten the wet patch on his groin. He is years away, at the wooden table in the big kitchen of his parents' house. It is Saturday. The stone walls keep the room cool, even on a hot August day like this one. They have finished lunch: cold ham, broad beans from the garden and Marthe's homemade brown bread. He and his father have embarked on Kurt's weekly science lesson. They are reviewing Newton's Laws of Motion when something crashes on the wall behind. They turn simultaneously, father and son, an echo of profiles. At the back of the kitchen, Kurt's mother is smashing her Hungarian wedding crystal.

It explodes against the wall, the kitchen tiles. Particles of crystal fly, glittering and white, like handfuls of new, powdery snow. Kurt sees a single fragment fall in the dog's water bowl. Marthe, their housekeeper, runs in and out again.

Kurt's father sighs, turning back to his son's diagrams and tapping them with the point of his pencil. 'Your mother gives us a useful case in point. Kurt? Are you listening? No, look at me. Newton's laws do not rule out the possibility of each glass your mother now throws at the wall reassembling itself and leaping back into her hand for her to return it to the shelf. "For every action, there is an equal but opposite reaction." Yes? Ah, I see the frown. My only son thinks I take liberties. But wait. We'll return to it. For now, tell me this. What does this seeming reversibility of action *also* suggest? What is the other implication, Kurt . . . ? No? I will tell you then. It suggests that time too, *in principle*, is reversible.

'Consider this, my boy. We know time only as the unfolding of events, yes? We have no other means of understanding it in practical terms. If an event were to fold back on itself, so too should time insofar as we understand it. But do not forget: either way, backward or forward, time – or the metaphorical flow of it we read for time – is illusory. That means invented, Kurt. Made up. Yes? If there is only space-time, and the best minds of this century tell us there is, why might effect *not* precede cause?'

Kurt is embarrassed that his father talks while his mother cries – or is he embarrassed that his mother cries while his father talks? She is behind them still, her hand a fist around the stem of a glass, her face like a piece of crumpled fruit.

'Perhaps,' Dr Zucker continues, 'perhaps if we could see beyond – could really see beyond – the convention of chronology, Kurt, perhaps if you and I and Mamma could believe, could *know*, that this Christmas we will again toast the season with the clinking of the Hungarian crystal, the necessity of that future event, the *certainty* of it, would operate as cause and bring both pressure and precision to bear on the atoms that constitute the shards of crystal that are now scattered on our floor. The inevitability of *that* event would effect a transformation we, in our ignorance, could only think magic.'

As always, Kurt falls in love with the sound of his father's voice. It is assured. It rolls on, like a drum roll, promising something. He ceases to care about his mother breaking glass and crying.

'And this is the thing, Kurt. The First Law of Thermodynamics does not constrain the glasses in any way that rules out them assembling themselves and jumping back miraculously into your mother's hand. Are we agreed? Good. So where would that energy come from, you ask? Where? Well, you tell me, Kurt.'

Another glass shatters against the wall.

His father taps his forehead. 'Think, Kurt. Think.'

'From the energy the glass has gained in flight?'

'Exactly. So what then is the difficulty for our Christmas toast? Why will we be drinking from paper cups this year? What stands between us, Kurt, and the reversibility of time?'

'I don't know.'

His father frowns. 'Last week. Remember Maxwell and Boltzmann? Remember thermal equilibrium?' He looks up, sees a cut on his wife's face. 'Never mind. Let's return to the facts of your mother's wedding crystal. The energy each glass gains from falling must go somewhere, yes? There must be an equal but opposite reaction of some kind. So where does it go? What happens? It goes into *heat*, Kurt, does it not? The atoms in the glass fragments and in the floorboards are moving around just a little faster now than they were before. The glass and the wall and the floorboards will be *warmer* than they were a few minutes ago. And yes, this heat energy is, in theory, just enough to raise all your mother's glasses and return them to the shelf, one by one. So what is the problem, Kurt?'

'The motions of the atoms are too messy to coordinate themselves?'

'Precisely. Heat is simply uncontrolled particle motions – and, as far as we know, uncontrollable particle motions. So it is heat that makes the motions, the events, of this life irreversible. It is heat, ultimately, that creates the illusion of the flow of time. Why? Because where there is heat there is entropy, and entropy knows only one direction. It is the world running down. It is manifest disorder. It is your mother's wedding crystal in pieces here on the floor.'

Dr Zucker puts down his pencil and closes Kurt's notebook. He brushes the lunch crumbs very carefully from the table into his hand. He pushes back his chair. 'Next Saturday, son. Yes? Next Saturday.' And Kurt watches him recede down the corridor, crumbs still in the fist of his hand. When he looks back to his mother, curled in a chair by the window, he says nothing. He can only stare at her, as if she is an intruder in the cool kitchen hush.

That first day, Ron expected body bags. He was prepared for body bags. Black Spunbond shells laminated with polyethylene film. Or maybe the heat-sealed PVC type, better if there are body fluids. He'd seen them often enough in his father's embalming room. He did not expect crates. He did not expect heavy-duty, zip-lock freezer bags. He's standing by his truck with the guy from Health & Safety. 'Body bags, mostly, just weren't feasible,' he's saying to Ron.

'Sure, no, I understand.' Ron hoists the crates slowly, loading the rear compartment first, bag by bag: segments of limbs; a finger with a ring on it; an ear; a toe; handfuls of soft tissue; three testicles; a foot in a shoe. He signs the dispatch form for Health & Safety. He nods when the guy mentions the counselling services available on and off site. Then he slams the DuraSeal doors against death and climbs into his cab.

'And I thought the hearse was heavy to steer.' James McLelland is sitting in the passenger seat, hands firm on his knees. 'How many miles you do to the gallon?'

Ron rolls his eyes.

'Seatbelt, son.'

He reaches for his belt, shifts into gear, and waits for someone to move the security barriers.

'So what they doing for a morgue, Ron?'

'Hangar B. At Shearwater.' Ron negotiates a tight turn, glad to be moving at last.

'In 1912, it was the Mayflower Curling Rink on Agricola Street.'

'I know.'

'Thought you'd have your own fleet by now. Somewhere hot. Somewhere far from here.'

'Nope.'

'Neil's done well for himself, hasn't he? Those pre-planned funerals seem to be taking off.'

'Yup.'

'He and the family going to Florida again this winter?'

'Guess so.'

'Linda fine?'

'Fine.'

'And the girls?'

'Fine.'

'I'm not gloating, Ron.'

'Right.'

'We are what we are. And we McLellands, we're ushers, Ron. Like midwives are ushers – or used to be anyway before the damned hospitals took over. They often came in families too, if I recollect rightly. It's a privilege, Ron.'

'I'm volunteering. A couple of days. Maybe a week. That's it.'

'Time's a switchback sometimes. You have to go backwards to go forward again.'

'If you say so.'

'Time doesn't need my permission, Ron.'

'Mind if I turn on the radio?'

'How many lost out there?'

'Two hundred and twenty-nine.'

'Won't be easy.'

'You don't say.'

'They'll start with distinctive marks and so on: a tattoo, an old fracture that might have been screwed together. Jewellery helps, of course – rings, watches and so on. Dental records will narrow it down a little. Footwear too, where they can make a match. Do you know what the airlines can't afford to tell you? Keep your passport in your shoe – that, I'm told, is your best chance of an early identification. Next, it's legs and arms. After that, well, it's down to the large intact remains of what we call "no visible anatomical character". That's legs which could be arms; arms which could be legs.'

'They've got DNA testing these days, Grandad. So let's change the subject, okay?'

'I'm not being morbid, Ron.'

'You do a good impression.'

'I had a life looking death in the face, and I'll tell you this. A bit of the living always go with the dead. It's two-way traffic, Ron. And I was proud to know that. It's you, you and your supposed sensitivities, that's what makes a morbid thing of it. You're so afraid of the stink, you know nothing else.'

'Not just the stink, Grandad. The wreckage. The debris. Do you know I've just put a bag in the back labelled "incomplete infant". Ever seen one of those?'

'You and your dirty mind again, Ron McLelland. Body parts. You into that? Is that what's on your mind? Well hear this, my boy. There's no such thing as parts. Or wreckage. Or debris. Because no one and no thing is ever separate. There's a whole-ness, Ron. That's right. A wholeness. Go ahead. Smile if you want to. But only the stupid and the young know no better, and Lord knows you're not so young any more. Now' – James McLelland suddenly claps his hands on his thighs – 'all that said, tell me this. Where can a dead man get a cup of tea around here?'

In the sea of her bed, Ginny wakes with a jolt. She runs naked and half asleep out of her dreams, out of her room, down the corridor, then stops short. She can hear only the gurgling of water in the radiators. It was a siren somewhere that entered her head and metamorphosed into the ringing of the phone. There was no call. No one was phoning. She goes back to bed, cold.

Kurt looks at his watch. Sixteen past nine New York time, an hour since take-off. Hal's meal tray is already empty, his Coke glass empty. He seems to doze. Kurt eyes the phone once more. He is reaching for his wallet when a flight attendant's voice interrupts the programme. She announces that the captain has switched on the seatbelt sign. The flight, she explains, is to be diverted to Halifax, forty-eight kilometres away. A small electrical fault is suspected. It is not a cause for concern. However, the captain has decided it would be prudent to correct it before beginning the long haul over the Atlantic. In the meantime, the cabin lighting will be switched off, purely as a precaution. Attendants will collect meal trays with the aid of flashlights. The in-flight entertainment will resume once they recommence their journey out of Halifax.

Sometimes, in the shower, on the subway, or in the line-up at his local deli, Kurt dreams of the entropic disclaimer, of the loophole that will allow him to undo the wild kinetics of heat and roll time back. He would like to be able to say to Ginny, 'I am not going to New York without you.' He would like to say to his mother long ago, 'You cut your face. Does it hurt?'

Hal comes out from under his earphones and taps Kurt's elbow. 'What do you make of that, Kurt? Halifax. Where *is* Halifax, for Pete's sake?'

The pretty stewardess with the mole on her cheek collects their trays. The cabin is dark, except for the bobbing beams of light. She says, 'We'll be landing soon. Could you straighten your seatback, sir?'

Somewhere, a baby cries. Just ahead of him, Kurt can see a white flutter of hands: Joan's patting John's. To his right, a heavy-set man in his sixties holds a small dark bag embroidered with gold thread, and turns it over and over again in his lap.

In the darkness of the cabin, people speak in low tones, as if in a foreign church, while far below them, Brenda Murphy is doing the crossword at the kitchen table in her mobile home. Now and again, she reaches down without looking and gives Lucky a good scratch. She glances at the clock. Twenty past ten. And still one clue she cannot get. 'A ten-letter word for "fate", Lucky. Then I'll let you out. It's not "destiny". Too short. The first letter is "p" and the sixth is "d" – at least it's a "d" if twelve down is "DiCaprio", as in "Leonardo".'

In the days to come, Ron McLelland will read and reread the timetable of disaster in his morning paper. He will plot in his mind the routine of his own movements that night, implausible now in their banality. He will see himself putting out the garbage, locking the front door, shutting the girls' bedroom door, and curling up next to Linda's just-bathed talcum smell. He will mark time against the movement of a clock that moved two hundred and twenty-nine people out of time.

10.00 Co-pilot smells smoke in cockpit. Checks. Finds nothing.

10.10 Smoke confirmed as the MD-11 widebody plane crosses the coast of Nova Scotia.

10.14 Captain radios Moncton Area Control Center. 'Swissair 111 heavy is declaring Pan, Pan, Pan.' Situation serious, not desperate. 'We'll divert to Boston.'

'Swissair 111, we'd suggest Halifax. Boston is three hundred nautical miles away. Halifax is seventy.'

'Confirm Halifax.'

10.16 'Ladies and gentlemen, the captain has switched on the seatbelt sign. We regret to inform you that this flight will be diverted to Halifax, forty-eight kilometres away. An electrical fault is suspected. It is not a cause for concern. However, the captain has decided it would be prudent to correct it before continuing our journey over the Atlantic. In the meantime, the cabin lighting will be switched off, purely as a precaution. Attendants will collect meal trays with the aid of flashlights. We thank you in advance for your cooperation.'

10.18 'What do you make of that, Kurt? Halifax. Where *is* Halifax, for Pete's sake?'

'Swissair 111, you've got thirty miles to fly to the runway.'

'We need more than thirty miles.'

'Turn left to lose some altitude.'

'Roger, we are turning left to heading, uh, north.'

'We'll be landing soon. Could you straighten your seatback, sir?'

'Swissair 111, when you have time could I have the number of souls on board?'

'Halifax, we must, uh, dump fuel. May we do that in this area during the descent?'

'Linda, is it the recycling tomorrow or just the garbage?'

'Recycling's on Wednesday, Ron. You ask every week.'

'Uh, okay, I'm going to take you – are you able to turn back to the south or do you want to stay closer to the airport?'

'Okay, we can turn towards the south to dump.'

'John, it doesn't matter. Just try to close your eyes until we land.'

'If necessary, sir, we'll put you up in a hotel overnight.'

'See, honey. I said that, didn't I?'

'Hal. Hal Huskins. Nice to meet you.'

'Bernie Rothenberg.'

'An electrician would come in handy about now, eh, Bernie? How are you on wiring?'

'As my dear wife would be quick to tell you – Hal? – Hal, I never was the handyman type. I'm a retired Hebrew teacher.'

'Turn to the left heading of two-zero-zero degrees and advise me when you are ready to dump. It will be about ten miles before you're off the coast. You're still within thirty-five, forty miles of the airport if you have to get here in a hurry. I'll advise you when you are over the water. It will be very shortly.'

10.20 'A ten-letter word for "fate", Lucky. Then I'll let you out.'

10.23 'Halifax, our autopilot is gone. Going over to manual.'

'Roger. You're almost there.'

'Kurt, you awake? This is Bernie. Bernie's an expert Hebrew teacher.'

'A *retired* Hebrew teacher.'

'Kurt's a physicist. Particular to particles.'

'What about you, Hal? What is it you do when you're not several thousand feet in the air?'

'Well, Bernie, I could lie but what the hell? I'm told by people who assure me they know that I'm what's called a "fantasist" – no, really, no kidding. A few years back, I took a stab at white-collar crime, failed – failed so badly I wasn't even arrested – then went crazy the next day in Central Park with a butterfly net. Landed myself on a doctor's couch. No, don't be embarrassed. Like I say, God knows I could have lied if I'd wanted to.'

10.24 'Swissair 111 is declaring emergency. I repeat, Swissair 111 is declaring emergency.'

'God, you're freezing, Ron. You didn't go outside in just your robe again, did you?'

'Who's looking, Linda? Jesus, it's cold out there tonight. Enough dew on the grass to sink a boat. Neil call today?'

'My biggest problem, Bernie, has always been believing everything's possible – and that's actually more limiting than it sounds.'

'Roger, Swissair 111. You're off coast.'

'We – dump. We have to land immediate –'

'No. But he's your brother. You could call him for a change.'

'Swissair 111, you are cleared to commence your fuel dump on that track. Advise me when the dump is complete.'

'Swissair 111 check. You're cleared to dump.'

'He said he'd phone me. Anyway, there's no point –'

'I repeat: you are cleared to dump.'

At twenty-five past ten Swissair III disappears from radio contact. In the tower at Halifax, two hundred and twenty-nine lives condense to a single pulse on the radar screen. In the starless night over St Margaret's Bay, the plane has begun its descent, spiralling like ticker tape in the air. It will be five minutes more before Brenda Murphy opens her door at New Harbour Point and marvels at the luminous mist of the September sky.

'My God,' Kurt mutters. 'We're going down.'

'Always good to have a physicist on board, Kurt. Now listen to me. Here's your life jacket. Remember the security position? Bernie, you okay? Grab your life jacket. Don't blow it up till you leave the plane. It's under your seat. Go on, Bernie.'

'Thank you, my friend. But I suspect this will suffice.' Bernie shakes out a wide piece of fringed cloth. 'My prayer shawl. I stuck it in my carry-on at the last minute.'

'There'll be an inflatable chute, Bernie, lifeboats, plenty of room, high-intensity flares till the Coast Guard arrives. Are we over water? We could be over water. Trust me. I used to work as a Security Adviser for United. In no time, you'll have the Gideon Bible in one hand and a stiff drink from your minibar in the other. Me, Bernie, I'll be stealing souvenir towels by morning. Kurt, you okay? Kurt?'

Overhead, compartment doors spring open; bags, boxes and coats fly into the darkness of the cabin. Flight III is in the jaws of sudden gravity.

John's head is on Joan's lap. 'I'm right here, right here,' she murmurs. 'We're okay, you and me. Always have been, always will be.'

'For Christ's sake, Joan, I can't hear you!' he cries. 'My ears. I can't hear you!'

Bernie wraps himself tightly in his shawl and bows his head. He moves his lips in fast, hot prayer as smoke billows in from First Class.

Oxygen masks do not drop.

'Kurt? Talk to me. You okay?'

Kurt feels a surge of hot urine between his legs. He is alone. Ginny is far away, asleep, and he is alone. He is rigid in his seat, strapped into circumstances, into an unbearable privacy. He feels he will burst with the sudden pressure of loneliness; that he will collapse under its immitigable force; that the crush of it, and not sudden impact, will, any moment now, take his life.

In their bed, Ginny turns, caught in a falling dream she will not remember.

Ron switches off the bedside light and gathers Linda to him, letting her warmth become his, while, in the closeness of the near night, a wing bursts into flame.

'Go on, Lucky. Go on.'

Heat rises, unknowable, infra-red. It is the heat of crackling circuitry and burning steel. It is, too, the ineffable heat of life in extremis: of Hal's desperate butterfly-net faith in a tomorrow that will not come; of Joan's twenty-five-year love for a man who could not love. It is the heat of Bernie's prayers for his wife's milky-white breast, shadowed with tumour – only now does he understand what she could not quite tell him over the phone at the gate. It is the heat of Kurt's sudden longing to press himself to his wife, to slip inside her, to make of their bodies a new third. It is radiant heat that rises high into the atmosphere.

Brenda Murphy looks into the night sky above St Margaret's Bay, wonders at something bright, alive, on the dim horizon between sea and sky, and, in that still moment between moments, in a moment that will be lost in the next, feels as porous as the mist is to the light; feels herself dissolve into something bigger, wider.

Then, 'Here, Lucky. Here, boy. Come on with you. It's late now.'